HIDDEN WITH YOU
J. KENNER

NEW YORK TIMES BESTSELLING AUTHOR

HIDDEN
WITH **YOU**
J. KENNER

"I saw her by the bar a few moments ago." Ollie grinned. "You can't miss her. She's wearing a gold mini dress. Like something out of an old James Bond movie."

Anticipation tightened Jasper's chest as the woman in gold filled his mind. *Zelda.* "Well," he said, "I look forward to meeting her." He shouldn't. He wasn't at this party—hell, he wasn't in this town—looking to get laid. And yet the first emotion—the only emotion—that had filled his head when he'd seen her was desire.

Not good.

He was in the States for one reason only. To locate and kill the man who'd murdered his family. He needed to stay focused, not fuck around or get distracted by women. Not even if a fast fling might take the edge off. Not even if the woman had piqued his interest in a way he hadn't felt in over a decade.

The woman was trouble, and if he knew what was good for him, he'd give Zelda Clayton a very wide berth.

**Charismatic. Dangerous. Sexy as hell.
Meet the elite team of Stark Security.**

Shattered With You
Shadows Of You
(free prequel to Broken With You)
Broken With You
Ruined With You
Wrecked With You
Destroyed With You
Memories of You
Ravaged With You
Hidden With You
Charmed By You
Tangled With You

———

**Meet Damien Stark in the New York
Times and international bestselling
series that left readers breathless…**

He'd pay any price to have her…
release me
claim me
complete me
take me (novella)
have me (novella)

play my game (novella)

seduce me (novella)

unwrap me (novella)

deepest kiss (novella)

entice me (novella)

anchor me

hold me (novella)

please me (novella)

lost with me

damien

indulge me (novella)

delight me (novella & bonus content)

cherish me (novella)

embrace me (novella)

enchant me

interview with the billionaire

Stark International Novellas:

Meet Jamie & Ryan-so hot it sizzles.

Tame Me

Tempt Me

Tease Me

Touch Me

For reading order and all JK titles, please visit
www.jkenner.com

HIDDEN WITH YOU

J. KENNER

NEW YORK TIMES BESTSELLING AUTHOR

M&O

Hidden With You Copyright © 2022 by Julie Kenner

Excerpt from *Release Me* © Copyright 2012 (used with permission from Bantam Books)

Cover design by Michele Catalano, Catalano Creative

Cover image by Annie Ray/Passion Pages

ISBN: 978-1-953572-53-0

Published by Martini & Olive Books

V-2022-4-24P

PROLOGUE

I'm no stranger to being alone. To being surrounded by people, but entirely by myself. Wrapped in darkness, yet hiding it with bright smiles and bubbly laughter. Faking a life in the hope it will become real but knowing that won't ever happen.

Then he entered my world, stepping past the walls that surround me. Filling the dark, small place in which I hide with light and hope.

He's here and he's real. He's sunshine and joy. Light and love.

But that is only an illusion. The truth is he belongs in the darkness. It feeds him. Fuels him.

He's horrible.

A monster. A bastard.

I look at him and know that's what I should think now that I know what he planned. What he wanted.

And yet there's warmth under his icy exterior. There's hope in his eyes.

I see it. I crave it. And somehow the monster turns beautiful in my sight.

But the more his heat engulfs me, the more I am afraid.

Because I know better than anyone that fire destroys everything, and all I can hope is that love can still bloom from the ashes of those flames.

CHAPTER ONE

J asper Kent sat on the bottom step of Jamie and Ryan Hunter's back porch, his toes in the sand as he watched the sun slip away. A few clouds hung low in the sky, now illuminated in vibrant shades of purple and orange as Mother Nature painted yet another masterpiece on the Malibu horizon.

This was what he'd dreamed of so many years ago. A home outside of London with a beautiful view where he could grow old with Sandra. A house where Bonnie could grow up, huge and roomy and ready to be filled with sisters and brothers for her. A fairytale life wherein he and Sandra would sit on the porch and watch their children play and laugh and grow. The world would continue to turn with its horrors and tragedies, but his family would stay warm and safe in the protective bubble of a loving home.

And how much of a crock had that turned out to be?

Instead of London, he was living in Los Angeles.

Instead of a family, he was all alone.

Instead of a home, he had a hotel room.

Instead of a life, he'd become a ghost.

No. Not a ghost. A hunter. For ten years, he'd been chasing the monster who'd murdered his family. That was his quest. His mission. That was why he'd left MI6 and gone freelance, sliding into a dark world where he killed for both money and information, taking out evil as he pursued his own vendetta.

For ten years, he'd chased lead after lead, but his efforts had led nowhere. Now, though, he had another. Thin, true, but it was all he had, and he would tug on this thread to the end.

That was why he'd come back to the States. Why he'd accepted the offer from Stark Security. He needed access to the well-funded agency's databases. He needed resources. Because with a decade of misses piled up behind him, he knew damn well that this was his last shot at finding the bastard who'd ripped Sandra and Bonnie from him. Screw this up and there'd be no retribution. No closure.

They'd be gone. Finally and truly gone.

Then he really would be a ghost. A haunted man, moving through the world, stripped of purpose and desire.

But not yet, dammit. Not quite yet.

He stiffened at the footsteps behind him, his training kicking in, then immediately relaxed as he recognized the gait. Ryan Hunter, the director of Stark Security and his new boss.

"You have an incredible house," Jasper said without turning around.

Ryan chuckled, then sat beside him. "And that's why we hired you. A man with eyes in the back of his head is handy in our business."

Jasper glanced over his shoulder and met the other man's piercing blue eyes. "And here I thought it was my good looks and sharp humor."

"That and Quincy's recommendation," Ryan retorted. Quincy Radcliffe, a former colleague from MI6, had left the service years ago. Jasper had heard rumors that he'd been involved in a vigilante group founded by billionaire playboy Dallas Sykes, but that seemed so unlike Quincy that Jasper had discounted the intel. Then again, the world was full of strange things—Jasper himself was proof of that— so maybe it was true. All he knew for sure was that Quincy was one of the first agents recruited to Stark Security by its founder, billion-aire Damien Stark.

So when the possible trails to his family's killer petered down to one narrow path leading to the States, Jasper had made a call. Quincy had intro-duced him to Damien and Ryan, and just like that, Jasper had a solid base in the States from where he could run his own operation. While doing the job they paid him for, too, of course.

"We don't have sunsets like that in London," Jasper said, gesturing at the pyrotechnics that were wrapping up in front of them, seemingly lighting the ocean on fire. Soon, darkness would fall completely, and the only illumination would come from the upper patio where the party was starting to ramp up as more and more guests arrived.

"We ordered it especially for you," Ryan said. "Wanted you to feel good about accepting this job."

"You certainly know how to roll out the red carpet." He turned to face his boss. "Seriously, thank you. It was time to leave London. Time for a change." That had been his excuse. The well-rehearsed explanation that after so many years, he needed to leave the memories behind. He could hardly tell his new boss that not only would his attention be split, but that he also intended to covertly utilize his new employer's tech to follow that precious, single lead.

Ryan nodded, his expression compassionate. "Come on. You already met Jamie, but Zelda's just arrived. And this party's just as much about her."

"Sounds good." He stood at the same time Ryan did, then shrugged into his jacket before bending down for his shoes. He slipped them on, then glanced once more at the infinite ocean. The light was gone, and the world hung in shades of gray. The same gray that had enveloped him since

Sandra's and Bonnie's light had been stolen from him. His wife had been thirty. Their daughter only five. Two entire lives gone, and he'd never get them back.

But somehow, someday, he would avenge them.

He turned his back to the gray, then followed Ryan up the wood and stone staircase that led toward the twinkling fairy-style lights that illuminated the upper levels of the huge back patio, and with each step he told himself he was getting closer to his goal.

***

"We're so glad you could make it," Jamie Archer Hunter said as she squeezed his hand and flashed a very camera-ready smile. She was the kind of woman the camera loved, with her sculptured face, wide mouth, and thick, dark hair. He knew she'd worked as an entertainment reporter and part-time actress before finally landing solid roles, including the lead in the upcoming *Intercontinental*, a thriller based on a book written by the other guest of honor, Zelda Clayton.

They were on the top level of decking by the infinity pool. The house was designed with four levels of decks, the top one partially covered with huge glass doors that could be fully opened. During the day, the view must be incredible. At night, the stars twinkled above, the house far enough away from its neighbors to welcome the darkness and invite starlight, making this outdoor living space warm and inviting and beautiful. Jasper could only assume the interior of the home was equally remarkable.

"I hope you didn't feel obligated to come," Jamie added, "what with being the new guy and all. This really wasn't intended to be a command performance."

Jasper laughed, immediately liking this woman. He'd heard that she said what was on her mind— most often unfiltered—and he appreciated the honesty. "Truth? I heard the house was completely remodeled by Jackson Steele, so I wanted to see it. And, of course, I wanted to congratulate you on your movie."

"Liar," she said with a laugh. "About the movie. I believe you about Jackson."

He grinned. Jasper was a long-time fan of the renowned architect's work. A man who also happened to be Stark's half-brother.

"We completely lucked into this house," Jamie said. "The former owner ended up moving away. A family thing. And then Damien mentioned to Ryan that it was going on the market, and we had Jackson come over to suss out the potential." She shrugged. "So now we live next door to our best friends. It's pretty awesome." Her smile rivaled the sky's brightest stars.

"At any rate," she continued, "I'll give you the

tour later, or feel free to wander inside. Jackson did a freaking amazing job." Her mouth twisted, and she rolled her eyes. "Did you hear that? I really just said *freaking*. That's me censoring my language even when there are absolutely zero kids around. Yo, Nicholas," she shouted to a lovely blond woman he recognized from various photos as Nikki Stark. "You and your brood have ruined me."

"I've got news for you, James," Nikki called back. "You were already ruined."

She shifted as she spoke, the movement just enough for Jasper to catch a glimpse of a woman passing behind her. The vision wore a dangerously short metallic-gold dress, her brown hair pulled up in a messy bun, the flickering lights catching some strands and making them glow red.

Inexplicably, he took a step forward, pausing when she disappeared behind a cluster of guests. *Who was she?*

"—totally right."

Jamie's words startled him, and he shook himself, mortified at his almost physical reaction to the woman in gold. He tried to think why—she hadn't reminded him of Sandra. She was pretty enough, but not breathtakingly beautiful. She didn't look the slightest bit familiar.

And yet damned if there hadn't been a tug.

"I lost you," Jamie said with a laugh. "Oh, god, I've turned into a boring hostess. I never would have believed it."

"You? Never. I just saw—"

She waited for him to finish his thought.

"I don't know," he confessed. "Possibly someone I knew." That wasn't it, but it was the only thing that sounded plausible. "Lost her in the darkness and the crowd."

"Well, we'll have to find her, won't we?"

He could practically see the gleam of matchmaking in her eyes, and since that was absolutely *not* on his agenda, he scrambled to change the subject. "Did I hear you call Nikki Stark *Nicholas*? And she called you James?"

"Oh, totally. Childhood nicknames."

"You grew up together?"

"In Texas, yeah. And you're from the UK. You don't have much of an accent. I would never have guessed if Ryan hadn't told me."

"Born in Manchester, but we moved to Manhattan when I was two. My father worked at the British Consulate in the city. I moved back to Britain to attend Oxford and ended up at MI6. I like tea, and *bloody hell* is my go-to curse. So I managed to fit in."

Her eyes twinkled. "I'll tell Ryan he got it all wrong."

"Great. Get me in trouble with the boss in my first week."

"Speaking of bosses, have you met Damien yet?"

He shook his head. "Ryan hired me over the

phone. When I came back to the States last month, I started out in Manhattan. Familiar territory. Besides, I understand Damien isn't in the office day to day."

"Yeah. He's got fingers in a lot of pies."

"I only started on Friday," Jasper told her. "And that was really just paperwork. Monday will be my real first day."

"Damien was gone all last week, anyway," Jamie told him. "Family getaway. They have a place in Lake Arrowhead. But he's great. Not nearly as intimidating as you'd think from the packaging."

"Is that so?" Jasper wasn't easily intimidated, but he'd watched interviews of the former tennis pro turned tech billionaire, and the man was formidable. Still, Jasper glanced around for a glimpse of the man, hoping to meet him soon.

He didn't find Damien in the clusters of people scattered across the various patio levels—nor did he find the woman in gold. Not that he'd been looking. Well, not too hard, anyway.

Nikki caught his eye, however, then came over, a tall man with an easy smile beside her. "I would apologize for Jamie," Nikki said to him, "but there's really no excuse for her." She extended her hand, clearly trying not to laugh as Jamie rolled her eyes. "Nikki Fairchild Stark. It's a pleasure to meet you."

"The pleasure is all mine," he said. She had sea-green eyes and wavy hair that fell to her shoulders in loose curls. She was girl next door pretty, and he remembered reading that she'd competed in pageants as a teenager. Now she ran a software development business, though most people outside of the tech world probably remembered her as the woman to whom Stark had paid a million dollars for a nude portrait. A scandal that started what had apparently turned into a very strong relationship.

The man with her wore jeans and a gray Henley, suitable for the casual party. The way he held himself wasn't casual, though. He stood tall, shoulders back, wavy hair in perfect order. He wore glasses, through which he was studying Jasper. His earlier smile had turned into a small frown at the corner of his mouth.

"Problem?"

"I'm sorry," the man said, apparently realizing he was staring. "I've been trying to place you. Have we met?"

Jasper shook his head. "I don't think so." Actually, he was certain; he had an almost infallible memory for faces. "What's your name?"

"I'm so sorry," Nikki said. "I should have introduced you."

"I'm Orlando McKee," the man said. "But call me Ollie. I've been friends with these two since the beginning of time."

"Jasper Kent. Just met them, but I expect we'll be friends to the end of time."

"Good answer," Ollie said, extending his hand

to shake. "Your name doesn't ring a bell, but damn, your face is familiar."

"Crossed paths through work, maybe?"

Ollie shook his head. "I don't think so. I used to be a lawyer. Was in private practice for awhile here in LA, a bit in Europe."

Jasper shook his head. "Fortunately, I haven't had the need of counsel." Except in dealing with the aftermath of Sandra's and Bonnie's deaths, but he wasn't going to mention that.

"Now I'm with the FBI," Ollie said, then grinned. "Maybe I've seen you on a Most Wanted poster."

Jasper chuckled. "No, I'm far too careful with my criminal activities for that. Former MI6, so I know how to be invisible." All true. Which, as Jasper knew well, was the best way to frame a lie.

"Well, it's a mystery. The only one I know from MI6 is Quincy." He shifted his attention to Jamie. "Is he here?"

"He and Eliza were heading down to walk on the beach when I saw them last. But they might have come back without me noticing."

"I'll go find him and introduce you," Ollie said.

"No need," Jasper said. "Quincy and I go way back."

"There you go," Jamie said. "You two have something in common. Do I know how to do hostess duty, or what?"

As Nikki laughed, Ollie gave Jamie a sideways

squeeze. "You're the Hostess Queen," he assured her. "But I think the queen is supposed to mingle."

"He has a point," Nikki said, her face alight with amusement.

"I suppose I could use another drink and a fresh round of gossip. Come on, Nicholas. Let's go find our husbands. These two can talk manly things."

With a smirk, Nikki followed her friend into the depth of the party. "So what'll it be?" Ollie asked. "Cigars? Car racing? We could stand around scratching our balls, nothing more manly than that."

Despite himself, Jasper laughed. Then even harder when Trevor, an agent he recognized from Stark Security, joined them. Trevor's brows rose as he put his hand on Ollie's shoulder and asked, "Did you really just say that? And way too loud?"

"I was being an ass," Ollie said, taking a casual step to the side and breaking contact. "It's my hobby."

"I'm going to go find a Scotch," Jasper said. "Because that's damn manly. Then I'm going to track down this writer—Zelda?—and congratulate her. Then I'm heading to my hotel and turning in. I'm still on London time." He wasn't, but he'd had enough socializing for the month. Sandra had been the one who loved parties. She'd made them fun. Now if he enjoyed himself for an hour, he considered it a stellar function. Beyond that, it was nothing but grueling work.

Tonight, Jamie and Nikki and the architecture itself had made the evening enjoyable. Better to leave on an up note.

"I saw her by the bar a few moments ago." Ollie grinned. "You can't miss her. She's wearing a gold mini dress. Like something out of an old James Bond movie."

Anticipation tightened Jasper's chest as the woman in gold filled his mind. *Zelda*. "Well," he said, "I look forward to meeting her." He shouldn't. He wasn't at this party—hell, he wasn't in this town —looking to get laid. And yet the first emotion—the only emotion—that had filled his head when he'd seen her was desire.

Not good.

He was in the States for one reason only. To locate and kill the man who'd murdered his family. He needed to stay focused, not fuck around or get distracted by women. Not even if a fast fling might take the edge off. Not even if the woman had piqued his interest in a way he hadn't felt in over a decade.

The woman was trouble, and if he knew what was good for him, he'd give Zelda Clayton a very wide berth.

"—she wouldn't come."

Jasper frowned, unable to play back Ollie's

words. "Sorry," he said. "I missed that. What were you saying?"

"That I'm glad Zelda came. When Ryan suggested to the two of them that they should co-host a celebratory party, she almost said no."

"I suppose some authors are uncomfortable in crowds," Jasper said.

"True," Ollie said. "But that wasn't the reason for Zelda. I think she was afraid her stepfather would be here."

"Ollie..." There was a hint of warning in Trevor's voice. "You really shouldn't—"

"It's not a secret," Ollie retorted, then shrugged. "But okay, yeah. It is gossip. Sorry."

"No problem," Jasper said. "But I admit I'm curious." He shouldn't be, dammit. He should excuse himself and go get a drink. Chatting about the lovely author was an absurd exercise.

Ollie eyed Trevor. "Fine," Trevor said. "Like you said, it's hardly a state secret. Zelda's stepfather is a Stark Security client. Carter Malloy. He's former CIA, and he runs a private security company."

"A client? Sounds like a competitor."

"Not really. Stark Security tends to do more investigative work, providing support for government agencies, stepping in to help private citizens when the authorities have turned away. That type of thing. We do take on protective services, but usually there's a personal connection between someone at the agency and the client. And those clients are usually smaller, whereas Malloy provides coverage for royalty and politicos on a regular basis."

Jasper nodded. "Got it. But what does that have to do with Zelda?"

"She can't stand him," Ollie said. "She's never said so publicly, but it's obvious. And he's a client, so Ryan couldn't not invite him."

"So where is he?"

"Europe somewhere," Trevor said. "He and Zelda's mom. That's when it changed from a party for Jamie landing the role to a party for the two of them. I'm glad, honestly. Zelda's pretty cool. Malloy's an ass, but he's an ass who pays the bills, and—"

"And now you really are in gossip territory." Ollie frowned at his friend.

Trevor shrugged it off. "Hey, Jasper's one of us now, right?" he asked, his inclusion of Ollie making Jasper wonder if the FBI agent was also working with the SSA. He didn't ask, though. Not now. Not when Zelda was filling his thoughts. A woman whose vibrant presence had grabbed his attention and whose tragic story had twisted his heart.

A woman he really needed to avoid.

Which begged the question of why he was suddenly excusing himself, then walking across the decking as he searched for a flash of gold in the crowd.

CHAPTER TWO

"Listen, Ms. Clayton, I know this isn't a book signing, and I'm not supposed to be fawning, but I just have to say how much I loved—like really, really loved—*Intercontinental*."

"Are you kidding?" I say, grinning at the cute blond guy. "You can toss praise at me any time. But you have to call me Zelda, okay?"

Jamie and I are standing in the middle of a semi-circle of guests—no press, thankfully, just friends and acquaintances and business associates, most of whom I've never met. Still, everyone is excited about the upcoming film, and Jamie and I are soaking up the praise and enthusiasm.

I glance sideways at her, flashing my best Party Girl smile. "See? I told you the book was popular. She thought she was signing on for a dud," I add to the crowd, grinning when they all laugh on cue.

Right now, I'm in my element. Or, at least, it

looks like I am. I can do the Perky Public Figure thing with the best of them.

"Yeah, because Jamie so often picks a dud," the cute guy says with a chuckle.

I glance between the two of them, realizing that of course she knows this guy. She and Ryan organized the party, after all.

"This is Eric," Jamie says, answering my unspoken question. "He works with Nikki."

"I do," Eric says. "And I read a lot of thrillers, and this series is one of my favorites. I'm looking forward to the next Martin King adventure."

"I'm very glad to hear it. Thanks." I flash him one of my best smiles, trying to discern if he's doing the fanboy thing or the flirting thing. And trying to decide which one I'm hoping for. I mean, he's cute enough, and I have no intention of going home alone, but all things being equal, I'm hoping the dark-haired guy I'd noticed earlier seeks me out. The one who filled out his jeans so perfectly and looked deadly hot in his white crew neck tee and casual black blazer.

He'd been standing on the lowest step leading down to the beach. The same place I'd been heading, needing a moment to ratchet down the joy. I play a good game in public—all bubbly and delightful in the role of the lighthearted heiress with the golden typewriter—but it's an exhausting role to play. I'd wanted a few moments of watching the sunset. A few moments to be alone. To be me.

But there he was, filling my space.

At first, I'd been irritated. Then he'd moved, and I'd been intrigued. As I watched, he kicked off his Sperry boat shoes, then moved off the step and slipped his toes into the sand. He peeled off his jacket next, the movements as he draped it over the handrail accentuating the muscles in his arms and back. I sighed, relishing the way his T-shirt stretched across his shoulders. His hair was cut short, so I could see the back of his neck, and despite myself, I imagined how it would feel to put my hand there and let the bristles from his close-cropped nape tease my palm.

I didn't go to him, but I didn't turn back either. Instead, I slipped off my shoes and held them by the straps as I slid under the handrail. Once my feet were in the warm sand of the dune, I crouched lower, knowing that if he turned around, I'd be hidden from his perspective by the support post.

I'm glad I took that precaution, because a few moments later, he glanced over his shoulder. As he looked toward the house—and me—I got a good look at his face, the visage eliciting a satisfied sigh. The guy was definitely something, with deep-set hazel eyes, a wide mouth, and the kind of sculpted jaw that only looked better with his hint of beard stubble.

The sun hadn't yet dipped below the horizon, and I saw a hint of gray at his temples, which did nothing to reduce his hotness factor. On the contrary, it made him seem even sexier.

I guessed he was in his early forties, which made him almost twice my age. Not someone I'd normally be attracted to, but there was no denying the way my pulse had kicked up. It was as if he'd physically reached out and touched me, and I stood frozen in my hiding place, afraid he was going to see me, and equally afraid that he wouldn't.

A heartbeat later, he turned away, once again facing the riot of colors Mother Nature was painting on the horizon. Then he took a seat on the step, moving with the kind of confident precision that most people drop when they think they're alone.

I stood frozen for a moment, debating whether I should go talk to him. Did he know I was there, or was he the kind of guy who was always in control, never letting down his guard even when he was completely alone?

Foolish, maybe, but right then, I wanted nothing more than to go to him. And I'd just convinced myself that I should when I heard someone coming. *Damn.*

I ducked down further, only to see Ryan Hunter pass by, his feet inches from my nose. I waited until he reached the guy, then slipped back onto the stairs and darted barefoot up to the top level, hoping my sunset-watching stranger hadn't noticed me, but still kind of hoping our paths would cross at the party.

The memory washes over me in a flash, and as I smile at the group and stand by Jamie, I let my eyes skim over everyone that I can see on this level of the patio. But I don't see my stranger anywhere.

"When will filming begin?" The question comes from someone near Jamie, and she answers, but I'm not paying attention until she says, "Zelda loves it."

"I'm sorry?" I say. "What do I love?"

Her brow furrows, and I realize she must be talking about writing. Because she's right. It's my life—what I love. Writing stories, sharing them with the world. Talking about them until the people around me are bored out of their mind, and then rejoicing when I find fans who are fascinated by my characters, my process, my made-up world. All the stuff that makes up the non-reality in which I live.

"I was just saying that you love the world that Martin King populates," Jamie says, referring to the hero of the series.

"Oh, yes, I do. He's got serious balls," I say to laughter all around.

"When's the next one come out?" someone asks.

"Knowing Zelda, it will be soon," someone shouts in reply, and the crowd titters. "She's a machine."

I force a chipper smile and a laugh, but this is

the uncomfortable part. When you first hit the *New York Times* list at seventeen, then have five more bestsellers between then and now—which happens to be the ripe old age of twenty-three— some people get really weird. Like they think I'm a total fraud who's been writing her books in crayon.

Or maybe I'm just touchy.

I shift the conversation to praising the screen- writer who wrote the adaptation. She's not at the party—instead she's in Manhattan having quality time with her family—but I describe some of our conversations, and how much care she took to understand the characters, and on and on, until I'm not listening to myself. It's just a hum of noise, and I'm the one doing the buzzing.

"Is it true you wrote *Intercontinental* in two months when you were only—" someone begins to ask, but I'm not in the mood to talk about my age, my break-out book, my family, or anything at all, really.

"Sorry," I interrupt, pressing my fingertips to my temple. "Light-headed. I've been going a mile a minute." I flash a winsome smile, like the little soldier doing her duty. "I should probably track down something to eat and sit for a bit. But I promise this one has all the answers," I add with a nod to Jamie, who frowns as if I've grown two heads. An understandable reaction. We've done a few public events, and usually I feed off the crowd's enthusiasm. Or seem to, anyway. But until today, no one at our joint events has jumped on the age thing.

I start to turn away, and she reaches for my arm. "Are you okay?"

"I'm fine. I just didn't eat today." A lie. My childhood bestie was in town overnight, and I'd met her for brunch before she hopped a plane back to Ohio. I'd been so excited to see her, but the truth was the brunch had been awkward. Full of long pauses interrupted by inane conversation, like we were meeting each other for the first time or something.

I'd gone home depressed and in no mood to party.

Which probably explains why my Perfect Party Girl manner isn't actually working out as effusively as I'd expected.

I need food. And alcohol. And a few moments alone to regroup.

"Find me later," Jamie says, and I nod in agreement, then flash my brightest smile and offer a finger-wiggle wave to the group.

"I'll be around," I say, "so if you want to talk thrillers or whatever, just track me down. Ply me with drinks, and I'll tell you everything." My voice doesn't sound as bright and shiny as I'd been going for, but I think I pulled it off, and with one final flash of my cheeriest smile, I turn and slip around the group clustered behind us and talking local politics.

Since that sounds like death masquerading as conversation, I pick up my tempo and slip inside the house right as one of the caterers is coming out of the side door that leads to the breakfast area.

I've been to Jamie's new house twice now, and I pause long enough to skim mentally over the floor plan. Then I slowly grin and hurry deeper into the house to the best place I can think of to be absolutely alone.

CHAPTER THREE

H*e was chasing a mirage.*
He'd caught an enticing glimpse of gold
in the distance, standing beside Jamie as if holding
court in front of a cluster of guests. He watched for
a while, mesmerized by the way she spoke and
laughed with the crowd. Then he'd been side-
tracked by Ryan again, and by the time he'd
reached the group, that blur of gold was long gone,
like water teasing a dying man in the desert.

Damn.

Now he shifted directions entirely, then
crossed to the opposite side of the massive porch,
finally stopping by two women sitting on the edge
of the hot tub and sipping wine.

"Have you seen Zelda Clayton?" he asked, but
the women only shook their heads, then returned to
their conversation about dates gone wrong.

"I mean, there was nothing romantic about the silences," one said. "Big. Gaping. Pauses at dinner. Not a thing to talk about."

As Jasper walked away, he wondered what he'd talk about once he found Zelda. Nothing came to mind, but it didn't matter. He was on a quest now. A foolish one, perhaps, but a quest nonetheless.

The last time he'd put so much mental energy into tracking a woman, it was because he'd been hired to kill her. She'd deserved it. She'd murdered her parents and husband for an inheritance, and his client—the husband's sister—had been wracked with both grief and fury when the bitch had been allowed to go free, with no criminal charges brought at all.

But while his target's ill-gotten inheritance might have bought her freedom from a corrupt judicial system, it hadn't been able to buy her protection from the grieving sister-in-law.

Once he'd completed the job, his client had inherited the fortune. And, as promised, she'd donated every last penny toward housing and healthcare for abandoned children in the UK and adults suffering from Alzheimer's.

As for Jasper, he'd used his extremely large fee to fund his own investigation, finally tracking down an unidentified woman whose picture had been sent to him by an anonymous source, along with a scribbled note: *Find her. She knows.*

It had taken years before he'd finally been able to confirm her identity as Melinda Barrett and locate her in London.

Melinda hadn't known much, but with her information, he'd forged the next two links in the chain that had drawn him to the States. Now he was trying to track down a sleazy, retired book-keeper named Tarlton Raleigh. A man about whom Jasper knew next to nothing. Only that he'd retired somewhere in America. That, at least, was a start, and Jasper intended to put Stark Security's excellent resources to work for him.

With luck, Raleigh would give him the second link that would lead Jasper to finding The Maestro, the shadowy sick fuck of a human who was Jasper's ultimate prey. The dead man walking who had killed his family. Who'd made them suffer.

And against whom Jasper was going to extract sweet, painful revenge.

He exhaled, letting the memory and anger flow out of him. Today wasn't about retribution, and Zelda had nothing to do with his family's death. She played no role in his mission. Yet there she was, filling his thoughts. And damned if she wasn't a welcome distraction from the pain and loss and memories that usually weighed him down.

And so he was going to find her. Touch her. He didn't know why it was so important. He wasn't prone to infatuation, and he didn't believe in fate.

But something about her had called to him. She'd become a talisman. If he could find the elusive woman in gold, then surely he could also, finally, track down The Maestro.

"Or maybe you're just losing it, Kent," he said, only realizing he'd spoken aloud when he heard the chuckle behind him. He turned to face Quincy Radcliffe and his wife, Eliza.

"I always said you were a bit mad," Quincy said, even as Eliza pulled Jasper into a hug.

"It's so great to see you again," she said, offering him the wide smile he remembered from the few times he'd joined her and Quincy for drinks in London's financial district. "Let me guess," she continued, pulling away with a stern expression, softened only by the gleam of amusement in her sky-blue eyes and the tease of the dimple in her cheek. "You were never really in finance either."

Jasper eyed Quincy. "I always told you she was both smart and a keeper. And no. I wasn't in finance. I served in MI6 just like your husband."

"So you left Queen and country to work for the SSA?"

"Actually, I left years ago. Been working free-lance security." He didn't mention that he'd been working primarily as an assassin, using the extremely high fees he commanded to fund his search for the man who murdered his family. Not a career choice he talked about, but he needed the cash. And he was very selective about the jobs he accepted, taking cases only where the justice system had failed and a vile criminal was walking free.

Considering the rumors about Quincy's former work with an organization called Deliverance, Jasper was sure his friend would understand. Eliza, however, might not.

"Congratulations, by the way," he continued. "I heard through the grapevine that you two had found each other again after my idiot friend here bailed on you. I'm really glad."

"Me, too," she said as Quincy drew her close in a way that made Jasper's heart ache. He'd had that once. A love that was both easy and intense, sweet and wild, deep and all-consuming and painfully, wonderfully real. A once-in-a-lifetime love that he would cherish always. He'd never feel that way again, he knew that. But as a vision of Zelda filled his thoughts, he knew that at least he could take the edge off.

He took a step to the side, intending to make some excuse so that he could continue looking for the gold-clad writer, but then Quincy lifted his hand in greeting to someone approaching from behind. Jasper turned, hoping it was her, only to find himself looking at a green-eyed man with dark blond hair and a surfer's build.

"Simon Barré," the surfer said. "You're the new guy?"

Jasper shook Simon's extended hand. "Looks that way."

"Well, that makes two of us."

"You're new?"

"I'm the newest field agent. But I've been at the SSA for awhile. I'm pretty settled in now."

"Settled?" Quincy chuckled. "At work, maybe. But I'm not sure he'll ever be settled here. Although I am impressed you came to this party. Or are you just a masochist?"

Simon narrowed his eyes, scowling at Quincy. But there was humor there, too.

"What's the joke?" Jasper asked.

"Los Angeles. Hollywood," Quincy said. "Our man Simon's not a fan."

Simon scowled. "I like the weather. I like the beach. I hate the industry. And I'm not particularly fond of the people who work in it." He shot a glance toward Jamie. "The breed, anyway. Some of them are tolerable."

"And yet there's San Diego," Jasper said. "Orange County. But here you are."

Eliza laughed. "You just met him, and you're already trying to get rid of him?"

"Just analyzing the contradiction that makes up the man."

"Don't even try. I'm a walking enigma." Simon flashed an easy grin. "Speaking of, have you seen Owen?"

Quincy shook his head. "Wasn't expecting too, though."

"Owen?" Jasper asked. He'd been scanning the deck to find Zelda, but the unfamiliar name caught his attention.

"New guy," Simon explained. "Not in the field. His area's research and analysis. Former CIA, apparently. Quiet. Sharp as a tack. But you want to talk enigmas..."

Since Jasper had zero interest in talking about any enigma that didn't center on how Zelda had seemingly managed to disappear entirely from her own party, he excused himself then took off toward the bar. In his experience, bartenders tended to be an observant lot, and that proved true when he asked the woman at the bar if she'd seen Zelda.

"Oh, the writer? Sure," she replied, passing him the bourbon he'd asked for. "I saw her go inside about ten minutes ago."

"Thanks." He followed the direction in which the bartender had pointed and found himself at the glass door that led into the breakfast area off the kitchen. He passed a caterer holding a tray of appetizers and continued inside. A few people from the party were sitting at the round table, and their presence alleviated what little guilt he had about wandering uninvited through Jamie and Ryan's home.

That guilt ramped up a bit as he left the kitchen area and entered the home's living spaces.

As far as he could tell, no one from the party had wandered this far in, and even after peeking into a room that turned out to be Ryan's home office, he still had no clue as to Zelda's whereabouts.

He was retracing his steps back to the breakfast area when he realized what he had missed. A small hallway off the kitchen. He followed it, then found himself at a glassed-in atrium, one side with a view of the ocean, another of the garden at the side of the house and the fence that separated the property from its neighbor. The third wall opened onto the master bedroom, and the final onto the large room in which he was standing, presumably intended to be some sort of playroom if the dart board, ping-pong table, and stereo system were any indication.

The wall seemed to be made entirely from a single sheet of glass, but as he shifted his angle, he saw a thin seam that turned out to be a hinged door, so perfectly cut that he would never have noticed the faint outline had he not been looking for a way in.

And he desperately wanted inside.

Not because of the beautiful, colorful garden that was spread out before him. Not because of the flowing fountain that served as a centerpiece. Not even because of the well-constructed stone path that wove its way through the exotic flora.

No, he wanted in because of the simple stone bench in the center—and the woman seated on it,

looking for all the world like a storybook princess
lost in the castle garden.

Zelda.

He'd found her.

As if he'd spoken aloud, she looked up, her eyes
locking on his. At first, there was no expression on
her face. She simply took him in. He felt his body
stiffen, as if preparing for a blow.

But then she smiled, that simple movement of
her lips making her radiant. He relaxed, soaking in
the warmth of her silent invitation as he moved to
the door and slowly pushed it open.

He let it close behind him, his body adjusting to
the warmer temperature and increased humidity. It
was like stepping into an erotic fantasy, lost in a
tropical paradise with a beautiful woman he craved.

Woman.

He paused, the word haunting him. She
couldn't be much more than twenty-two. Maybe
twenty-three. A girl, not a woman. At least not
compared to him. He'd turned forty-four last week,
so what the hell did he think he was doing fantasizing about this girl? This kid.

He'd seen her youth the first moment he'd
glimpsed her, the girl in gold. He'd seen it, and it
hadn't mattered. He'd only seen *her*. Only
wanted her.

But now, here in this fairytale world, what he
craved seemed ridiculous. Wrong, even. She looked

like an innocent princess sitting outside the castle. And he was hardly Prince Charming.

"Did you change your mind?"

The words were simple, and she offered no explanation as to what she meant. But he knew. He heard the part she hadn't said: *Did you change your mind about me? About what you want?*

He started to say that he had. That she might be of age, but she was still far too young for him. But when he met her eyes, he saw pain. Before, on the patio, she'd seemed to glow with energy and exuberance, like the Fountain of Youth incarnate. Now it was if she'd shed a costume, her youth stripped away.

He saw darkness now. The weight of a life that overwhelmed the years she'd spent on this earth. She was older than her years, he thought. And maybe she was younger, too.

"I don't know why I'm here," he said honestly.

"You've been watching me. You must have had a reason. That's why you came, isn't it?"

His chest tightened with the realization that she was fully aware that he'd been watching her. Then loosened again when he heard the full meaning hidden in her words: She'd been watching him, too.

He took a step toward her. "What if I told you I'm not sure why I came?"

Her smile was an invitation. "Maybe you came

to be alone, like I did. Maybe you came to be alone with me."

He knew he should just walk away. He had enough darkness; he didn't need to take on hers.

But he told himself there was no harm in talking. "Yeah," he said, taking one step toward her. "Maybe I did."

CHAPTER FOUR

I watch as he moves closer, and I try to hide my smile. It's hard, though. After all, he's here, isn't he? As if my will drew him to me. As if I have magical powers that allow me to bend the world to my liking.

I almost laugh at the thought, because god knows, if I had such powers, my life would be so very, very different. Still, he's here, just like I'd imagined he would be, and my body sizzles in anticipation.

At first, I wasn't sure he was going to stay, but now that he's made the decision, I wait for him to come to me. To say something else. But he's silent now, and though he crossed to the middle of the room, he hasn't come any closer.

He's waiting for me.

The realization is delicious, like he's candy-coated a perfectly choreographed romance wherein

I slide off this bench, our eyes meet, and I walk confidently into his arms, both of us meeting halfway.

But that's not what I do.

Instead, I stay right where I am. I might crave those fantasies, but I know better than most that the only place we can live in is reality.

And in this, he needs to come to me. Because how else can I know that this moment is real and not something I'm rewriting in my imagination?

I wait, my chest tight with anticipation, but he doesn't come any closer, and the uncertainty is almost painful. Has he stopped because he doesn't want what I want? Or has he stopped because my fantasy is also his, and he's waiting for me to come to him, and we'll both stay firmly rooted despite desire, like two lovers in an O'Henry short story?

I'm writing our dialogue in my head, trying to see where any possible thread could lead, when his voice, low and steady, fills the room. "Tell me why you're really here."

My brows rise in genuine surprise at the question. "I thought we were past all that. If we're going back to the beginning, shouldn't you start with hello?"

"Hello," he says. "Why are you here?"

"I told you. I wanted to be alone."

"And yet you invited me to stay. So why are you really here when the party in your honor is out there?"

I wait a moment to answer, mostly so that I'm
certain the delight I'm feeling won't escape in the
form of a laugh. I'm not entirely sure why I'm so
delighted—maybe because he's asking the very
question I want to avoid. Maybe because the question makes clear that he actually sees me. That I'm
not just some ghost floating through the moment.
Whatever the reason, his question fills me up. But
at the same time, I don't want to answer it, so I
parry with a question of my own. "Does it really
matter?"

He takes a step forward. Just eighteen inches or
so, but my entire body tenses in anticipation. "No. I
guess it doesn't."

He takes two more steps. Thirty-six inches. An
entire yard that had been separating us now gone.

"I'm not a people person," I say, but whether
I'm answering his question or commenting on his
increasing proximity, I really can't say. Probably the
latter. Ironic, I suppose. After all, while I'd been
outside of this glassed-in bubble, I'd done more
than my usual share of fantasizing about this
stranger's touch. Now that he's almost close enough
to make that fantasy come true, my insides are all
twisted up.

I thought I knew what I wanted.

Now, I just know that I *want*. And I'm nervous
as hell about getting it.

"Not a people person," he repeats, and I find I
can't take my eyes off his mouth. It's wide, with

full lips of deep red that accentuate his white teeth. It's an expressive mouth, too. I notice that much when his lips curve down into a frown. "I'm surprised," he says, and I have to play back the conversation in my head to remember what we were talking about.

"Why? You hardly know me."

"So let's get to know each other. As for the why, I saw you out there. Moving through the guests, you and Jamie talking to your adoring public."

I have to laugh at that. "Jamie's the one the public adores, and she adores them right back."

"You don't?"

"I love my readers. But being the center of attention? It's not my happy place. Really," I add, seeing the disbelief on his face. "I probably should have been an actress, because I can pretend with the best of them, but no. Bamboo under the fingernails would be a much better pastime."

"Then you really are an excellent actress."

He crosses the rest of the way, then sits on the bench beside me. We both shift so that we're facing each other, and when our knees brush, I'm suddenly, acutely, *sensually* aware of how close he is. Very, very much inside my personal bubble.

"As far as I could tell, you were perfectly at ease in that crowd," he continues.

"You watched me?"

"I already told you I did."

"Right. You did." I'm flustered, and I'm afraid it

shows. "I just meant—oh, hell, I don't know what I meant."

"You mean that I watched *you*." He slides a bit closer as he speaks. "I wasn't listening to the questions or the answers. I wasn't translating the sounds you made into words. I was just watching. You bewitched me, I think."

His cheek dimples when he smiles, something I hadn't noticed from far away since he sports a closely shaved beard. Right now, I'm obsessed with that tiny, kissable indentation, and it's taking all my strength not to reach out and touch it. Instead, I repeat, "*bewitched*," because it's the only word that has lingered in my head. And because at the moment it seems pretty damn apropos.

He shifts slightly, and his denim-covered knee strokes my bare one, this new movement sending an arrow of heat up my thigh and right to my core. I bite my lip, fighting to restrain a shudder of sensual pleasure right through me.

Maybe he'd bewitched me, too.

I clear my throat. "Funny," I say, trying to make my voice sound casual. "I didn't notice you at all."

His grin is slow, sexy, and ridiculously tempting. "Liar."

"I am," I say. "I'm an expert at weaving lies. Better be careful."

He reaches up and strokes the pad of his thumb along my jawline. "I'm always careful."

"I—I don't even know your name." I'm on

sensory overload. The way our knees are brushing. The lingering sensation of his thumb on my face. And now his hand is on my other knee, the tips of his fingers on the bare skin of my thigh.

I fight a ragged breath even as I fantasize about him sliding his hand higher up my leg. The short dress is designed for standing, and I'm showing far too much thigh as I sit like this. It would be so easy for his fingers to sneak under the dress. To tug aside the tiny thong I wore to avoid panty lines. I'm wet just thinking about it, and right then, that's all I want. For him to touch and tease me until I'm open and begging. For him to lay me down on this bench, yank my skirt up, and pound himself into me.

I want the excitement. The release.

I want the danger.

I want what I want, and then I want it to be over. Itch scratched. Time to move on.

That oh-so-common story, and one I seem to write over and over in the novel of my life. People leave. That's just the truth of it. They bring me joy, then take what they want. They suck me dry, then they leave.

Better to expect it. To relish the part that I want, then forget the part that I don't.

To not get close so as to not get hurt.

Even better, be the taker. Be the leaver. Because there's a hell of a lot less heartache that way.

Do it, I tell myself. And then, before I change

my mind, I put one hand on his, then ease his fingers up under my skirt. "Higher," I whisper as I cup my other hand around his neck, then pull his mouth down to mine. He doesn't resist. On the contrary, he makes this kiss his, claiming me with his mouth even as his fingers tease the inside of my thigh, so close to heaven, but still so far.

I want to beg, but his kiss is too deep, his hold on my head too tight. I squirm, silently begging for more, but even as I do, he's lifting me by the waist and settling me on his lap. The dress rides up, leaving my ass exposed, and he cups my butt cheek with one hand while his other hand fists my shoulder-length hair. It's wild and intense, and exactly what I need. Heat and lust and a pleasure so intense it will drown out everything else.

"Please," I murmur against his mouth. I rock my hips, feeling his erection through his jeans as my fingers go to the button of his fly. "Please."

He squeezes my ass, then twists the band of my thong, pulling it up from the back and making the material rub against my clit. I grind against him, wanting more, wanting to feel him inside me. Knowing this is too fast, and not caring in the least. He captured me from the first moment I saw him, and everything about this evening has been leading up to this connection, this building passion, this—

"No."

The vile word is a whisper against my lips, then

he pulls back, breathing hard. "I'm sorry," he repeats. "But no."

I try to grasp hold of reality, certain I understood him wrong. "You want this," I say, certain of the desire I see in his eyes. "We both do."

"Desperately."

"Then why?"

"Zelda." He says my name flatly, as if the answer was obvious. But, of course, it's not.

Then it hits me. "No. No, that's bullshit."

"I'm forty-four. What is that? Twice your age?"

"Not even," I say. Technically true, but I'm staying silent about the fact that I'm not quite twenty-four. "What does that matter? It's sex, not a relationship. And I am not my age."

He winces but otherwise keeps it together. "Maybe not. But I'm mine."

He slides me off his lap and onto the bench, then stands. I stay sitting, too angry to trust my legs to support me. Angry and frustrated and defeated. Because seriously What. The. Fuck?

I shove all my anger into my legs, forcing them to do their job as I stand, adjust my dress, and then march over to him.

"You think I'm some naïve college-kid? You have no idea. I've lived a full life and then some. I've seen things—done things—experienced things that—"

I cut myself off with a shake of my head. My personal traumas are not stories I wield to get a man in bed, and why it matters that this man knows me, I really have no clue. Because knowing is dangerous.

I'm not a girl who wants to get to know a guy. I just want the moment. The adrenaline. That sense of not being alone even when I am alone.

Which begs the question of why I'm fighting so hard for a fuck. Do I really care that much that he pushed me away?

Is my ego really that fragile?

Yeah. Apparently it is.

"You don't know me," I repeat.

"No," he says. "But I know me. And as much as I want this—and trust me, I *do* want it—it's not going to happen. I really am sorry."

Then he leaves. He just turns and walks out of the atrium, leaving me pissed and horny and angry.

And wanting him even more.

CHAPTER FIVE

I tell myself I shouldn't care, but when I return to the party and don't see him, disappointment settles over me like a gray fog. I turn slowly, looking for Jamie, because I think this is my cue to leave, too. I came here tonight in the role of the peppy and perky author, giddy about having her book adapted into a Major Motion Picture—the kind of deal wherein those words should be spoken by that guy who narrates movie trailers, then underscored with a drumroll and a cymbal crash.

In other words, hyper-celebratory.

Right now, I'm just feeling let down. Which is ridiculous, since I don't know anything about that guy other than that he was chatting with some of the men who work with Jamie's husband. I mean, hell, I never even learned his name.

I consider asking Jamie but decide against it. Jamie is wired to interfere. She gets even a whiff of a hint that I'm interested in a guy—even if only in a FWB kinda way—and she'll dive into matchmaker mode. Worse, she'll tell Ryan, and it'll probably get back to Mystery Man, and god only knows what kind of nightmarish web I'll end up entangled in.

Better to ask Leah. She's much more likely to keep a secret. She's a spy, after all. More or less, anyway.

Twelve years older than me, Leah Ramirez is the aunt to my elementary school bestie, Camille, who moved to Ohio with her mom the summer after seventh grade, and with whom I communicated in only monosyllables and grunts at brunch. But I've kept up with Leah, who spent many an evening and weekend babysitting both of us, and even stayed in my house for two months back when she was between apartments and my parents were out of town.

I'd been fifteen and hadn't wanted them to hire back my childhood nanny. Apparently in their mind, Leah made a good substitute, and after Leah moved out, neither my mom nor my stepfather, Carter, seemed to notice that I had the run of the house unsupervised except for the live-in housekeeper, Tricia, and other transient staff.

Leah and I keep in touch, though I'm sure she's probably just in the habit of checking on me. Everyone older than me has always checked on me, the poor little rich girl raised by the staff because her parents were too lame to hang around.

I grimace, irritated at the way my mind has spun off topic. Bottom line is that if I want to know about Mystery Guy without word getting back to him, then Leah is a good place to start.

Unfortunately, even though she works at Stark Security, Leah isn't at the party. I try to remember where she is—she'd gone out of town for work—but damned if I can recall where. Phoenix, maybe. Or Albuquerque. I remember thinking dry and dusty when she told me, but I wasn't paying too much attention.

Still, she has her cell, and I'll give her a call as soon as I get home. So long as it's before two, I know Leah will answer.

Then again, maybe I won't call at all. Maybe it's better I don't know the guy's name. Better I just let this infatuation go. Tonight, I'll write out in my journal the way I'd hoped the evening would go, full of every wild fantasy and erotic detail that comes to mind. Then I'll turn the page and move on with the rest of my life, same as I'd do with any other guy.

"You're leaving already?" Jamie asks when I finally track her down. She and Nikki Stark, along with my agent, Evelyn Dodge, have gone down to the beach, and now they're shoeless and chasing the waves, which cracks me up since Nikki and Evelyn are both the pulled-together type. Shoeless Jamie doesn't surprise me at all. Frankly, Naked Jamie wouldn't shock me.

"Come join us," Nikki says.

I start to decline, then decide what the hell. I kick off my shoes and race in, almost knocking Evelyn over in the process. "Whoa there, girl. I want to splash, not take a bath."

"Sorry." I adore Evelyn, especially since she took me on when I was just fourteen and a production company had come knocking, wanting to buy the film rights for *Twisted Destiny,* the serialized young adult fantasy I was writing that had generated a scarily huge number of fans. Even being raised the way I was—as in, surrounded by money and all it could buy—I'd been intimidated by the process. And since my mom and stepfather were both useless and absent, she stepped in to help with the process, even going so far as to get their power of attorney so that she could legally sign on behalf of Minor Me.

"I didn't see you up there," I tell Evelyn, nodding toward the decking and the house.

"I saw you," she says. "You and Jamie. You both looked good."

"I hate that part," I admit.

"But you do it anyway, and you do it well. So good girl." Evelyn's in her sixties, but you'd never know it by looking. She has a timeless kind of face, both strong and kind. She always says what she thinks, and the only agenda she ever pushes is her client's. My stepfather tries to get me to fire her every time he's in town, telling me she gets too personal and doesn't focus enough on the business side. But Carter's an ass, and from where I'm standing, Evelyn has helped build my business right alongside me, which is more than I can say for either of my parents.

"Is everything okay?" she asks me now, frowning at the way I've stopped chasing the waves, unlike Jamie and Nikki, who are laughing like crazy a few yards down the beach.

"Sure," I lie, because honestly, when has everything been okay?

"You were looking for me earlier. I thought maybe you needed something."

"What? Oh, no. I wasn't looking," I assure her. "I just meant that I didn't realize you were here. I was wondering about somebody I met."

"Oh?"

"Just a guy I chatted with. No big deal."

"Well, good for you," she says, which makes me frown.

"I'm sorry?"

"For not leaving with him."

"Are you kidding me?" I snap. "You're my agent, not my mom."

Her brows rise, and she crosses her arms. "The difference between me and your mother is that I care. *Shit*," she adds. "That was completely uncalled for. Too many bourbons tonight."

"No," I say. "It's fine. Hell, it's more than fine. It's true." I shrug. I know she thinks her words hurt, but they didn't. They're just the truth. And I've been dealing with the truth about my life for twenty-three years.

"I just worry about you," she says, and I sigh. She knows me better than anyone, and so she knows that I haven't had a boyfriend since fifth grade when Tommy Dean and I went steady for all of a week. Instead, I serial date. Or, more accurately, I serial fuck. Why not? The breakup will inevitably happen, so why not enjoy the good part and avoid the bad?

"You don't have to worry," I assure her. "It's all good. Haven't you heard? I'm an international sensation. Thank you for that, by the way."

Her mouth quirks into a half-smile. Evelyn is a shark at the negotiating table, and everything that's gone right in the trajectory of my career is because she had my back.

But that's my career. And while I'm grateful we're close, at the end of the day, my personal life isn't her business at all.

"Listen," I say, "I'm going to head out."

"So early?"

I shrug. "It's after ten, and you know me. I can take a crowd for only so long." I glance toward where Nikki and Jamie are huddled together, looking as if they're deep in conversation. "Tell them bye for me?"

"Of course." She pulls me into a hug. It's awkward—I've never been big on the hugging thing

—but it's nice to know she cares. I mean, I get that I'm a client, but that doesn't change the fact that it feels good.

With her final admonition to "drive safe" echoing behind me, I head back up the steps, then keep my head down as I make a beeline toward the gate that leads from the back patio to the front parking area. I'm not in the mood to talk to anyone unless it's my Mystery Guy. I'm tempted to look for him, but I talk myself out of it. He's the one who walked away, after all. I'm hardly going to press the issue. Because how pathetic would that be?

Apparently very pathetic, because even though I have been very firmly telling myself that I don't want to see him again, I'm still weirdly disappointed when I don't find him leaning against my car, like the first act turning point of a sexy rom com.

Guess that means I'm living a drama and not a comedy.

With a sigh, I slide into my Prius, telling myself that this is good. I didn't want to see him. I don't need to see him. There is no point in seeing him.

All of which—of course—means that I'm bummed about not seeing him.

Honestly, hormones are a bitch.

I crank up the radio to drown out my thoughts, then jam to a My Chemical Romance playlist as I race down the Coast Highway toward the 10, and then, ultimately, my house in the Platinum Triangle. Or, rather, my father's house. He'd left it in trust for me when he died, with a proviso that my mother could live there, too. Mostly, though, she travels, which is fine by me.

Even though she's rarely around, I don't live in the house. As far as I'm concerned, it's twelve thousand square feet of lonely rooms and way too many memories. Instead, I live in a guesthouse by the pool. I should probably suck it up and move into the main house—but I'm not quite ready to do that yet, so I use the living room as an office and the media room for watching movies. Tricia, the housekeeper who's been here since before my dad died, still lives on site with her husband, who's in charge of landscaping.

Someday, I might move back into that monstrosity, but thinking about it makes me sad and overwhelmed. So I don't. I live in my eleven hundred square feet, write my books, pay the bills necessary to keep a mostly empty house humming along, and try to forget about it.

Neither my home nor the main house are visible from the road, surrounded as they are by a huge row of hedges. I turn down our private drive, slow as I approach the gate, and smile at the wonders of technology as it opens just in time, triggered by the magical barcode sticker on my front windshield.

I follow the driveway around the main house, then park in the garage next to the classic Mustang convertible my dad had been rebuilding before he got so sick. It's under a dust cover, and every time I park my car, I tell myself I'm going learn about cars and finish what he started.

It won't happen, though. It makes me sad to let that reality settle in my brain, but I know it's the truth. I want the car to be complete—I want to get it there to honor my father. But I know myself well enough to know that even though I can play out the scenario in my head, I'm never going to watch YouTube videos on carburetors or slide under the car to work on the chassis.

I mean, I'm not even entirely sure what the chassis is.

So my dream of completing my father's last project is only that—a dream. Just one of the many fantasies that live in my head. That I might play out on paper but never, ever in reality.

I tell myself that's a good thing. Those stories are my work. My purpose.

Sometimes I even believe that.

Other times, like now, I think that I'm as naïve as some of the characters I write. And why not? They're me, too, after all.

I circle my car, then head to the garage side door. I hit the button to close the main garage door, then follow the stone path that leads to the pool, but I branch off to the right before I get to the tiled pool deck, and follow that path to my doorway.

I punch in my key code, then push open the

cottage door and step into the combination entry/living/dining area. I toss my purse on the sofa. As I do, I veer to the right toward the kitchen and notice the small stack of mail on the kitchen table along with a plate of chocolate chip cookies and a note that has no writing other than a smiley face.

I grin, take a cookie, and make a mental note to thank Tricia in the morning. Then I sort through my mail, most of which is either junk or bills. A letter-size envelope catches my attention, primarily because it has no postage.

I use a knife to open it, then pull out the single sheet of paper. There's a single word on it, printed in a massive font size: *YOU*.

Confused, I turn it over, then drop the paper and jump backwards as if it had suddenly morphed into a snake. The paper flutters down to the tabletop as my heart bounds behind my rib cage.

I draw in a breath and force myself to look down. To really see the all-too familiar image that my brain has already processed: the cartoon-style silhouette of a girl sighted in the target of a rifle.

And underneath that, smaller but still huge and bold, are two more words: *DEAD. SOON*.

CHAPTER SIX

H*e wasn't supposed to be wandering these electronic paths.*

Jasper glanced from the computer screen to the cavernous room filled with desks. It wasn't yet seven in the morning, and he'd been here since five. He'd been jolted awake at the climax—literally— of a seriously delicious dream starring him and Zelda Clayton. A full-color, X-rated dream that he had tried very hard to get out of his head so he could grab a few more hours of sleep.

That, however, had proved impossible. Instead, he'd taken a freezing cold shower, grabbed a coffee from the service area by the hotel's reception desk, and had the courtesy car drop him at the office, where he'd finally pushed Zelda out of his head by focusing on what really mattered—finding a killer.

Now, he twisted in his chair, stretching his back and looking to see who had come in while he'd been lost in his work. No one he recognized. Just a couple of guys sitting at the long tables devoted to research and analysis, and both seemed completely absorbed by their own work.

Good.

He exhaled, then turned back to his task of traipsing down the electronic paths through this government database, searching for any reference to either the bookkeeper, Raleigh, or the sadistic prick who'd actually killed his family. *The Maestro.*

He had to be here. A clue, a lead, something. Jasper's off-the-books, just-might-get-him-fired-on-his-second-day-of-work search into the bowels of the Stark Security computer system couldn't turn out to have been in vain.

Except after another thirty minutes of burning eyeballs staring at a screen, he still hadn't found either of the men. He'd risked his job and his reputation by using Stark Security's access to the data network for the SOC—the Sensitive Operations Command—a black ops organization that answered to the Pentagon. And if anyone there realized that he'd done so without prior authorization—and for his own personal gain—there would be some serious hell to pay.

It would be worth it. If it led to Sandra and Bonnie's killer, it would be worth any price.

Except, dammit, he'd found nothing.

A wasted risk and a wasted morning. Well, fu—

"Trouble with the database?"

Jasper had been working covert operations almost since he'd been out of nappies. Even so, he jumped a mile at the polite voice behind him. He turned around to find himself facing a lanky man with a bland smile and thick red hair cut so short he looked like a new recruit to the military.

"Trying to dig up some background on a case," Jasper said. He clicked off his monitor as he spun his chair around. "I'm Jasper Kent. Second day."

"I know." The man extended his hand. "Owen Porter. Research and Analysis. I didn't think you'd been assigned a case yet."

Jasper laughed, wondering if anyone would notice if he just broke Owen's neck and shoved him in the office supply closet. Probably.

Instead, he cleared his throat. "Yeah, nothing yet, but I'm looking to impress. Thought I'd see if I could make progress on a dead file. Probably a foolish idea. It's only day two. I'm sure I'll get a formal assignment today."

"Probably," Owen agreed, grabbing a rolling chair from the nearest desk. He plunked down in it, then rolled closer to Jasper. "But that's the kind of initiative they appreciate around here. Let me help you."

"Help?" He forced a smile. "Great. I mean, yeah, that would be great." Hell, maybe it would be. "But, um, I don't want to announce that I'm doing this, then have it go nowhere. Not the impressive result I want to present to the boss, you know?"

"Mum's the word," Owen said. "Honestly, I've spent the last week mapping coordinates so Linda and Winston can track a couple of smugglers across Europe. It's mind numbing, but I'm supposed to be focused. The thing is, I can only be focused so long before my brain melts. I need a break. You need help. Sounds like a recipe for success to me, and we both have reason to stay quiet." He flashed a smile. "Trust me when I say it's no more legit for me to access the SOC database than you without proper authorization on the file. I go in, and we really are in this together."

"In that case, Owen, by all means. Let's go to hell together."

"Come over to my desk," Owen said. "Nothing suspicious about me on their interface. But right now, about the only thing you should be investigating is—well, I can't think of anything witty, but do me a solid and pretend."

"Hell of a sense of humor you've got there," Jasper said, liking Owen more and more. He followed the analyst to his desk, pulled up a chair, and settled in.

By the time the office started to fill up around nine, he had two leads on a bookkeeper named Raleigh who'd recently relocated to the States. Even better, Owen had managed to find a reference to a known assassin who often used the codename

Maestro. No location—not yet—but Owen
promised to keep working on it.

"Thanks," Jasper said. "I mean it. I just might
end up solving that cold case and impressing the
boss."

Owen nodded slowly. "You just might. Of
course, you'll have something meatier to work on
soon, I'm sure. No reason to continue playing with
a cold case."

"I finish what I start."

Owen leaned back in his chair, those pale blue
eyes hard on Jasper. When he spoke, his words said,
"Good for you." His tone and his eyes said, *What's
the real story?*

Jasper waited for the man to voice that actual
question, and when he didn't, Jasper took a step
toward his desk.

"Hang on," Owen said.

Jasper drew in a breath as he took a quick
self-assessment. Only when he was certain he'd
give nothing away did he turn back around.
"Yeah?"

"There's overlap, isn't there?"

"What do you mean?" Jasper asked. He knew
exactly what Owen meant.

Owen hesitated before answering, looking
around to make sure that no one else was close
enough to hear. "Raleigh. The Maestro. There's
overlap with a case you had before. At MI6. The
one that got away, and I bet it's been eating at you.

So you pulled a cold case, told me there's a connection, and now you're digging in."

Steady. Steady.

He waited five beats, giving himself time to assess the possible repercussions of each possible answer. Ultimately, he decided on the truth. Or, at least, the version of the truth that Owen had concocted.

"You're very good at what you do," Jasper said.

"I'm an analyst. I analyze."

"And now? Planning a conversation with Ryan?"

"Actually, I'm planning on helping you. Assuming you want my help."

Jasper hesitated only long enough to really take this guy in. A shotgun assessment, but one in which Owen came out on top. "All right. Good. Thank you."

Jasper started to turn away again when Owen added, "They putting you up at the Stark Century?"

Jasper nodded. "For the time being."

"That won't last forever. Then you either have to foot the bill to live in one of this city's most expensive hotels, or you find another place to live."

"I've been checking message boards. I'm just looking for a room right now. No lease until I know the city better. Figure out where I want to live, although I'm already partial to the beach."

"I've got a place in Venice. Bedroom, bath, and

open area. Great porch." He nodded at a box of cigars on his desk. San Cristobal Ovations, an excellent brand with a beautiful brightly colored label featuring a parrot.

"Those came yesterday. Smoked them for years, then gave it up, but now I'm thinking a cigar, some whiskey, good conversation. You could come over one evening, check the place out, have a drink." He shrugged. "I'm new in town, too, so..."

"A cigar and a drink sounds great."

"Perfect. Second floor of my condo could be all yours. I could use a roommate."

"Really?" Jasper started to ask why—maybe Owen was just overly friendly, maybe he was lonely, maybe he was gay, but maybe there was something else going on. Before he could frame the question, he was interrupted by Ryan's voice from across the room.

"Jasper, with me. Grab your coat."

"Think about it," Owen said. "We'll talk later. In the meantime, I'll keep poking around. Chatter. Dark web. Whatever I can find."

"Good man," Jasper said, then snapped his computer off and hurried to follow his boss.

CHAPTER SEVEN

A hard rage ripped through Jasper as he clutched the threat—now sealed in a clear plastic envelope—tight in his hand. He felt like a spring, ready to lash out and pummel whoever had sent the vile note. But since that wasn't possible, he paced the short distance from one side of Zelda Clayton's living area to the other, trying without success to burn off some of his fury.

When Ryan first told them where they were going, Jasper hadn't been sure if the assignment would be a nightmare or a dream.

Then Ryan had filled him in on the threatening note. After that, there was no way to categorize this clusterfuck as anything other than a nightmare.

"This is Jasper Kent," Ryan had said when they'd first arrived, and in that moment, Jasper knew that he should have had at least another hour to prepare. Ten would have been better. Because there was something about this woman. Something that shifted him just a little off-kilter. And damned if he hadn't felt happy—*fucking happy*—to be there, even though the only reason he was seeing her again was that someone had threatened her life.

God, he was a prick.

Apparently she hadn't clued into the full extent of his asshole tendencies, because she'd reached out and taken his hand, hers soft against his calloused palm. "Nice to put a name to the face."

"You two met at the party?" Ryan asked.

"We chatted briefly," she said, then offered him a winning smile. "I'd hoped for more, but you know how parties are. I'm so glad to see you now, Mr. Kent. I feel much safer with you—both of you —here."

"Call me Jasper, please. Mr. Kent makes me sound like my father." He said the words firmly, wanting to remind himself why he'd walked away.

"All right," she said. "Call me Zelda."

He nodded, thankful for the way she was dressed. Sweatpants and a tee—nothing provocative in the least. And her hair hung in two braids over her ears. The style accentuated her eyes, wide mouth, and the smattering of adorable freckles on her nose. The style also made her look about sixteen. Which was just fine, he told himself. He wanted all the reminders he could get of the gap in their ages. Because thinking about that was a hell of a lot better than recalling last night's dream.

He cleared his throat, then held up the note. The side with the target and the word DEAD was facing him, and an icy fury formed in his veins. "Tell us again how you got this," he said, working to keep his voice level and businesslike as he faced Zelda. He shot a quick glance toward Ryan, checking to make sure his boss was genuinely cool with Jasper jumping into the thick of it.

On their way over, Ryan had said that he wanted Jasper to take point. "A way for me to get to know your personality in the field with a client." And wasn't it just Jasper's luck that the first client out of the gate was the only woman in years who had truly managed to get under his skin.

"It was in the mail," Zelda began, explaining how she'd come in to find the mail on her table.

You.

The words from the threat echoed in his head under Zelda's words.

"There wasn't postage, but I didn't think anything of that. Honestly, I'm not even sure I noticed until I saw the note and looked for a return address."

Dead.

How the hell had someone so easily maneuvered this threat into her home? How was that possible on this huge compound in one of the most expensive and presumably well-protected gated communities in all of the Los Angeles area?

Soon.

He was still trying to wrap his head around the reality of where and how Zelda lived, but he was having a hell of a time. It shouldn't be this hard. He wasn't awed by generational wealth or by the trappings of royalty. He'd visited much richer and more luxurious estates. But this private, new money home was palatial, and she didn't even live in the main house. Instead, it sat empty while she lived in a tiny guest cottage.

The whole situation was odd, and he wanted to unravel the mystery of where she chose to live and sleep as much as the question of who sent the note.

And he wanted to keep Zelda close while doing both.

She was still by the sofa, and he took a step toward her, then paused. He didn't want to get too close. Didn't want to risk her or Ryan seeing his thoughts. He might have walked away last night because she was too damn young, but apparently his subconscious was undeterred. His thoughts had stayed on her, only to surface last night in sensual dreams in which he'd touched her, tasted her, filled her. He'd awakened with a rock-hard cock and the taste of her pussy on his lips and—

"—come?"

"What? Sorry?" He jolted back to reality, his entire body on edge, both from the memory and the fear that any part of it had shown on his face. Or anywhere.

"I said that Tricia's back from the grocery store.

I can go ask her about the envelope, and did you want to come?" Her face didn't change. Not really. But he was certain he saw laughter in her eyes.

He cleared his throat and rolled his shoulders, stalling as he gathered his thoughts. "I'll want to talk to her, but presumably it was left in the mailbox or at the main gate into the subdivision. So I'll need to talk to the guard there, too. And look at your security feed. I presume you have cameras at the gate entrances to your property? How big is this place, anyway?"

"Yes to the cameras. And the cottage is only eleven hundred square feet. But the house is twelve thousand. Well, closer to thirteen, but I round down. I mean, the place is freaking huge," she continued, her tone managing to be both cavalier and awed, and he liked her all the more for it.

"We have ten acres total," she added. "There's a pool, a pavilion, a tennis court, a ten-car detached garage, a helipad, a small orchard, and a huge garden with a walking path. Oh, and the koi pond."

"All enclosed?"

She nodded. "A fence tied into the security system, and a hedgerow. And, yes, cameras." She shrugged. "You probably could have gotten all that from Zillow, but happy to help."

He shot a glance at her, then looked back down before she saw his smile. "Like I said, we'll want the security feed."

"You can have it," she assured him. "But I

already looked. I can access it all from my laptop. That's what I was doing before you came."

"And?" He glanced at Ryan to see if the other man had any comments, but his boss only lifted his phone, then motioned that he was stepping outside.

"Just you and me," Zelda said once the door closed behind Ryan.

"And we have work to do."

She took a step toward him. "Listen, Jasper. About last night..."

"We have work to do," Jasper repeated. "Important work to keep you safe. So tell me what you saw."

She drew in a breath, as if preparing for a new assault, but then her shoulders relaxed. "Fine. I didn't see anything, honestly. Nothing odd along our fence line, and the only car that stopped at our drive was the mailman. I couldn't see what he put into the box, but I can't imagine he'd deliver something with no postage. Plus, the envelope only had my first name and the street address. No city or zip code."

Jasper nodded. He'd noticed that as well. "My guess is that someone left it with the guard at the gate to the subdivision, and he brought it to your box himself or had a runner."

She nodded. "Exactly. I talked to Frank—he mans the gate most days. He said someone gave him the envelope and asked him to put it in our box. He was going to bring it up at the end of his shift, but when Dalton Carrol rode by, he asked him to do it."

"Dalton Carrol?"

"Next property over. He's training for some hundred-mile bike ride, so he rides every day. He usually stops and chats with Frank. I guess Frank's a biking fan, too. Watches the Tour de France and all that."

"Any bad blood between your family and the Carrols? Property dispute?"

"Nope. Not a thing. I think he just ended up being the delivery guy." She wrinkled her nose. "He's going to feel really shitty about that. Do you have to talk to him?"

"We'll see. What did Frank say?" He wanted to be irritated. To lecture her on the danger of going out in the world to play detective with a death threat hanging over her. And all of that was true. But the irritation was squashed by genuine respect. Whatever else she might be, the woman knew how to take care of herself. And she didn't spook easily. Probably came from writing thrillers and getting into the heads of her characters.

"Unfortunately, Frank didn't have a lot to go on," she continued. "It's not that uncommon for someone to drop things at the gate house. Invitations, documents that need to be signed or reviewed, even flowers. It's easier to accept things at the gate and then have a runner take it to the mailbox. Otherwise, they have to vet every delivery person they let pass, and that's a huge pain."

She shrugged. "Despite me being the object lesson in exceptions, security really is tight around here. Like stifling tight sometimes."

"In other words, Frank has nothing useful to tell us."

"Unfortunately, you're right." She turned her head, making her braids swing. "He thinks it was a guy, and he thinks the guy was wearing a ball cap. But he wouldn't swear to anything."

"What about the footage at the gate? It's still possible it was someone who entered the community legitimately. And statistically, most threats come from someone you know."

"That might be statistically true, but when you factor in the picture, I think it's someone who only thinks they know me."

He frowned. "What are you talking about?" he asked, then immediately held up his hand. "Wait. One thing at a time. The gatehouse camera feed. We need to request it."

She shook her head. "I already reviewed it, too. Frank gave me the log-in. Nada."

"No cars?"

"Only five cars in the last twenty-four hours that didn't already have a bar code, and nobody in those vehicles rang a bell with me. I know a few of the others, of course. They're neighbors. But we already know none of them stopped at our mailbox, driving or on foot."

She smiled at him, the bright and perky smile he'd seen her flash at the party. "Listen, Jasper, I called you guys because I wanted another opinion, not a full-on Secret Service thing. I mean, surely this isn't a credible threat, right? I mean, it's just some asshole playing with me."

"Why on earth would you immediately jump to that conclusion?" Jasper said, then did a mental rewind. "Wait. What did you mean earlier when you said that the picture means the sender is someone who thinks they know you?"

"It's just ... Well, I mean they're using my book."

"Your book?" He glanced sideways as Ryan re-entered the condo.

"What about your book?" Ryan asked. "And which one?"

"*Intercontinental.* The first Martin King book. The one they're making into a movie," she added for Jasper's benefit. "Hang on."

A huge bookcase dominated the southernmost wall, and she headed that way, then pulled down a thick hardback book. She flipped through it, marked a place with the dust jacket, then passed it to Ryan, who immediately opened and skimmed the text. "See?"

Jasper watched as Ryan finished reading, then flipped forward before looking up at Zelda. Jasper frowned, then crossed to Ryan and took the book, reading the marked page himself.

It was a threat using the exact language: *You. Dead. Soon.*

"Check the chapter heading. The graphic, I mean."

He did. It was a target with the silhouette of a woman dead center.

Jasper and Ryan exchanged glances. "This does make it seem like someone is playing with you," Jasper said. "Very specifically, too. But you sound almost cavalier about the whole thing."

She shook her head. "Oh, I'm not. I'm serious about wanting confirmation. I mean I could be wrong and I'm really not keen on dying. But if they really are using the book as a model, then the threat is only meant to scare me."

"Because that's what happened in the book," Jasper said, understanding dawning.

"Exactly. It wasn't a serious death threat at all. The victim gets the threat, but Martin learns that the guy who left it never intended to kill her."

She turned her attention from him to Ryan. "Don't you think that someone who really meant to hurt me would've had more balls? I mean, surely they know the plot, right? So, it's probably just some freak who's obsessed with me. But I don't think they actually want to hurt me. I think they just want to get my attention."

"Get your attention why?" Jasper asked.

Her brow furrowed. "Honestly, I don't know."

"It's a good theory," Ryan said. "But we're not taking chances."

"But—"

Ryan shook head. "No. We're not eliminating the possibility of a threat because of the way you plotted your book. You called because you're worried. Do you think Jamie would forgive me if I let you dismiss us out of hand?"

She sighed, then went to sit in an overstuffed armchair, her legs curled up underneath her. "I probably should have just let it slide. It's going to turn out to be nothing, and you're going to end up wasting time on me, diverting resources from clients with legit issues."

"No," Jasper said firmly. "You did the right thing. However this turns out, it's a legit issue. You're frustrated and scared. You want to believe this was just a prank, but more than that, you want to know the truth. You want answers even while you want to push it all away."

The moment the words were out of his mouth, he wanted to call them back. He knew too much about what she must be feeling. The need for answers when all you want to do is forget and walk away.

She met his eyes, and he saw understanding there. More than that, he felt that same zing of connection he'd felt last night at the party.

She didn't look away. And, damn him, neither did he.

After a moment, she licked her lips, then turned with visible effort to face Ryan. "So where does that leave me? Should I wear Kevlar? Hire someone to taste my food for poison? And honestly, if someone shoots me, it's only going to help the film. Hell of a publicity coup for Jamie and the studio. Hey, maybe she's our bad guy."

Ryan nodded slowly. "Actually, that's a solid thread to tug."

"Jamie?" Incredulity dripped from her voice.

"No," Jasper cut in, understanding what Ryan was thinking. "Not his wife. But this might be a publicity stunt cooked up by the producer."

Her eyes went wide. "Oh, please. You should be the one writing thrillers, not me. Your plotting skills are exceptional. But also way too over the top."

"Matthew Holt's company is producing, right?" Ryan asked. "We need to talk to him."

"There's no way that Matthew—"

"Not disagreeing," Ryan said. "I know him, too. But maybe one of his people decided to try to work some PR magic. A new hire, very gung-ho. And until we know for sure, you'll have someone from the SSA with you at all times," he added, pointing toward Zelda.

"You can't be serious." She glanced toward Jasper as if asking for help.

"Until we know there's no real threat, it's the safest thing." Jasper said, jealous of Leah or Emma or one of the other female agents who would surely be assigned.

"Meanwhile—" Ryan began, but the ring of his phone cut off his thoughts. He answered the call, listened, then ended it. Then he turned to Jasper. "Your things are here."

"Excuse me?"

"I had hotel staff pack up your room. Leah's at the gate with a small team to deliver them. That was the gatehouse, confirming access."

Jasper glanced at Zelda, who laughed.

"Something funny?"

"It's like your clothes are the Crown Jewels. An entire SSA team to transport them."

"Excuse me," Ryan said. "I have another call to make. I'll meet them at the driveway gate and send them in."

"No prob," Zelda said, then broke into a smile the moment Ryan was out of the cottage." "Looks like I'm not the only one trapped like a rat. The least we can do is make lemonade from the lemons."

"We're not going to be making anything."

"You regret it, don't you?" She took a step closer. "Admit it. You regret not touching me. You thought about it all night."

"You think a little too highly of yourself, Ms.

Clayton," he said, hoping she couldn't see the lie. "Quite the ego you have there."

She shrugged casually. "Only about things I know I'm good at."

He moved closer as an impossible thought slid into his head. "And what exactly are you good at? Seducing a man? Or maybe you're good at crafting a story?"

Her brow furrowed with confusion, only to be replaced by fury as the meaning of his words hit her. "What the hell is your problem? Are you really suggesting that I set this up? Like a giant hoax?"

When he didn't answer, she stalked forward, her face alight with fury. "That is fucking bullshit. And I wasn't the only one in that atrium. So don't you dare try to act all proper like I took your damn virtue or something. You were right there with me."

"I was," he said, studying her face. Trying to read her. To get inside that mind and discern what she was capable of. "Now here I am again, but this time I'm doing a job, and we will figure this out. We'll find who's threatening you." He took a step closer. "And it looks like I'll be right by your side until we do."

"I'm suddenly less excited by that prospect than I was," she snapped.

"Honestly? I think that's for the best." He was watching her face, looking for signs. Trying to read her thoughts. But he couldn't. The woman had remarkable control. And a temper. From the fury that flared in her eyes, he could only assume that he was saved from a stream of vitriol by Ryan's return.

"Well, you're all set," Ryan said, looking between the two of them as if unaware of the tension and temper filling the room. "And I'll reach out to Matthew Holt to set up an appointment for tomorrow."

"Sounds good," Jasper said as Zelda crossed her arms and glared.

"Jasper, you know the drill. You're her shadow. Hell, you're her conjoined twin, and you two need to work together to tease out possible suspects. And Zelda," he added, "I don't care how much you think this might be a hoax, it is still a threat, and we're going to take it seriously. So you two make a list of anyone and everyone who might want to harm you."

"Ryan—"

"No. There's work to be done, and you know it. We've talked about it enough when you wanted help plotting. Now you get to live it."

"Great. I'm so thrilled."

"Jasper, walk with me." Jasper did, following Ryan back to the front door, then outside where they could talk without the risk of being overheard. "Initial impressions?"

For a moment, Jasper considered staying silent about his theory. After all, in the years since he'd left MI6, he'd reported to no one but himself, and he trusted his judgment. And what his judgment told him was that she wasn't behind this. More than that, he knew that she'd be furious when she learned that he'd shared his hypothesis with Ryan.

But at the end of the day, he worked for Stark Security now. He wasn't a free agent, no matter what his motives were for accepting Damien and Ryan's job offer. He was using the SSA as a cover for his own investigation, but he was still doing the work they assigned him. And, dammit, he didn't have it in him to do a half-assed job.

"You're not going to like it," he told Ryan, "but we need to consider the possibility that she did this herself. A call for attention. Publicity for the movie or for her book. She might think it's terribly clever. And honestly, it would be. She's smart. She's smarter than I think most people give her credit for. Or maybe they give her too much credit. God knows she's accomplished a lot for someone so young. Maybe she thinks she can get away with anything."

For a moment, he thought that Ryan was going to argue. But then his boss nodded slowly. "I don't want to believe that of her. I like her, and she's been through a lot. But you're right about her being smart. And arrogant. She's accomplished a lot in a very short time against incredible odds. But the bottom line is that she's a sweet kid who's had it rough."

Kid. He needed to keep reminding himself that she was just a kid.

Ryan paused, then shifted as he looked at Jasper more directly. "This movie's been in development for two years, and Jamie met Zelda pretty early on. She reached out, asking if I'd answer questions to help her plot the next couple of books, and I did. And I got to know her a bit through those conversations. The Zelda I know wouldn't play the kind of game you're suggesting."

"So you want me to just drop the theory?" Jasper snapped. "Based on your gut?"

Ryan tilted his head, his expression so hard that Jasper almost wanted to recall the words. "The woman I just described is the woman I know. But you don't know that Zelda. Not yet. So you look at her through your eyes, and you find out who's doing this. And if it's her, we'll deal. But I damn sure hope that's not the way this turns out."

Jasper let out a slow breath. "Me too." The words were true. He barely knew the woman. But he couldn't deny that he liked her, too.

And a hell of a lot more than he ought to.

CHAPTER EIGHT

While Jasper and Ryan talk outside, I replay the conversation in my head. There was something behind Jasper's words, but I can't quite figure out what it was. He was pushing. Prodding.

Something is going on in his head, and all that I can think is that he's circling back to our time in the atrium.

I sigh. I want to tell myself that night was a mistake. That getting up close and personal with the guy—only to find out that he's my personal bodyguard—is not going to go well.

Still, I can't regret it any more than I can deny that I still want him. And it pisses me off that he's so close, and at the same time so out of reach.

When he walks back in, my head snaps up, and before I can censor myself, I say, "You shouldn't have left."

"Ryan and I had things to talk about. You may

be paying the bills, but sometimes we need to talk without the client around."

"That's not what I was talking about."

He studies me, and I feel my body tingle as his gaze roams over me. I'm watching his face, and I see heat rise in his eyes when he realizes what I mean. "You're talking about the party."

I lift my chin. "You should have finished what you started."

He doesn't say a thing, but I'm certain that when he speaks, he's going to shut this down. He'll tell me that I need to drop it. That anything physical between us would be unprofessional. And if I can't dial myself in, he'll have Ryan assign somebody else to watch over me.

Honestly, that's what he should do. That would be the professional thing to do. Ryan doesn't know what happened, after all. Or, at least I assume he doesn't. So Jasper will tell him, Jasper will be off the case, and that will be that.

He should do that. More importantly, I should want him to. I should want him gone, because the man twists me up inside more than he should. I know it's because of unfinished business. That promised but undelivered orgasm in the atrium.

It's not like I'm interested in anything developing between us, and I don't play out fantasies about guys in my head. I'm not that girl. And yet last night, I was. I did. I got home and spun fantasies in the dark with my hands and the memory of his face. His lips. His body.

"Well?" I snap when I realize where my mind has gone in the lingering silence.

He grins. "I'm not the one who started it. And, yeah, it is better that I walked."

"Better?" I move past him and into the kitchen area, needing to do something other than just stand there looking at him, wishing that he would touch me. I put a pod into the Keurig and start a cup of coffee brewing.

"I mean that I'm here now. And I need to stay objective. If we'd gone any further, objectivity would be out the window."

He's moved into the kitchen, too. I'm still facing my coffee, but I see him in my peripheral vision leaning against the half wall that separates the dining area from the galley-style kitchen. I want to turn around and look at his face, but I don't. Instead, I watch the stream of coffee dripping down into my cup. And I think about his words. *Objectivity.*

Objectivity? How does objectivity play into a bodyguard job?

For a moment, I don't understand, then I get it. And the realization feels as if he'd tossed my hot coffee right in my face. I whirl around to face him. "You prick."

His eyes go wide. "What the hell?"

I cross to him in two long strides. "You

goddamn son-of-a-bitch."

"What—"

"You think I had something to do with this. You think that I'm a suspect. That's what you can't be objective about. If you'd fucked me, then you'd be all lost in your hormones and couldn't look at me objectively. Well, damn it, Jasper, look. *Look at me.* Because I didn't do anything except end up with some son-of-a-bitch sending me a threatening note, and how dare you think otherwise."

I'm pacing now, fury coming off me in waves. He really thinks that I set this up? What kind of a bastard thinks like that?

"Damn it, calm down." He grabs me by the shoulders and holds me in place, trying to force me to face him. I dip my head, so that the only thing I'm facing is the tips of his shoes.

"Look at me."

I don't.

"Damn it, look at me."

I lift my head, seething. "I *do* want you to be invested. I need you to be invested. Do you think I want some anonymous rent-a-cop watching over me? Someone I don't know? I want someone who at least likes me. Someone who finds me interesting and actually likes that I'm on this planet. But no way in hell would I pull an elaborate scam to get you here in the first place."

"Zel—"

I hold up a hand and continue on, not even

pausing for breath. "I wanted you last night because you're hot. Because you caught my eye and set my hormones firing. Not because of some elaborate hoax. How the hell would that even work?"

I can see his temper flaring and take a step back. He just pulls me closer, so that we're only inches apart. "Did you do this? Did you set this up so I would end up here watching over you? Is this your retribution for me walking away? Some poor little rich girl with her psycho stalker, and I'm going to feel sorry enough to fuck you?"

My hand suddenly stings, and I realize after the fact that I've reached up and slapped him across the face. "Let. Go. Of. Me."

He does, and I shove him hard as I back away. "I just told you it wasn't, you fucking prick. How can you even think that?"

"How can I do my job and not think it? I don't know you. I just met you. I don't know a thing about you except that you have one hell of an imagination. And here's the thing, Princess, Right now, I'm working for you. I'm not sleeping with you."

I scoff. "Right now, I'm thinking that's a good thing."

For a moment, we only glare at each other. Finally, I feel my shoulders sag. "Did you really think that? That I could do that?"

His gaze stays hard for a moment, then his entire face seems to crumble. He sinks into one of the dining table chairs as if all the energy has been sapped from his body. "I don't know you, Zelda. I have an impression of you, and it's one that I like. I admire your talent and your drive. But what's inside you? I don't know that. And I've lived long enough to know that people are capable of hiding a hell of a lot of crazy behind the mask of their face."

I want to hate him for believing that of me. For not being able to look into my heart and see the truth of me. But I can't. He's right. I want to believe that despite all my dark places, that the whole world knows that I'm a good person. That I radiate some magical checkmark and shiny gold star.

I'm naïve and foolish. And today, maybe I was even a little bit cruel.

"I'm sorry," I say. "My feelings were hurt, and I overreacted. I don't like it, but I get it."

"Apology accepted. And for what it's worth, I didn't like thinking that way."

I flash him a hint of a smile. "Well, that's some-thing. And for what it's worth, I promise you, I didn't do this. Someone is ... well, honestly, I don't know what someone is doing. Maybe it's just a joke. Maybe nobody wants to hurt me at all. I don't know, but, dammit, I'm actually scared. I know it's not a real threat in the book, but this might be, and...." I stop talking, realizing that my throat is full of tears, some of which have actually escaped down my cheeks.

I look away. It's positively mortifying.

He comes to me, then cups the back of my

head. He pulls me close, and I lean against his chest and sob. "I'm sorry," I say when I can speak. "This isn't like me. I don't usually burst into tears. But I'm scared. I'm really and truly scared."

"I know. I believe you."

I tilt my head to look at his face. "Really?" He nods, and while he could be putting on a show to appease the possibly psychotic client, all I see is the truth there.

"Thank you," I whisper. And then, before I can help myself, I rise onto my toes and brush my lips over his. He responds, pulling me closer, his lips parting, the kiss moving from sweet to hard and needy. I moan, wanting so badly to finish what we started in the atrium, but as my hands slide down his back to cup his ass, he pushes me away, gently but firmly.

"I'm sorry," he says. "I shouldn't have let that get out of control."

"It's okay." I hear the plea in my voice and hate myself for it. "We both want it."

"Maybe. But we're not at a party anymore. I'm not just a guy you met. I'm working for you. I'm not going to sleep with you, too."

"No matter how much you want to?"

"No matter how much I want to," he says, acknowledging the truth.

"Well, thank you for that at least. Of course, I could just fire you, and that would fix everything."

The corners of his eyes crinkle with amusement, which only makes him look sexier. "That would be foolish. I'm good at what I do." He clears his throat. "And it's not just because you're a client."

"You think I'm too young."

"You are too young."

"I'm not really twenty-three," I say, and watch as his eyes widen. "I mean, in years I might be, but I'm older. Hell, sometimes I feel like I'm as old as dirt."

"Very young, very lovely dirt."

I grin. "I knew you liked the view." With a sigh, I move past him into the living area and go sit on the sofa. I glance at the other cushion, then up at him. He hesitates, then joins me, sitting far enough away that there's no risk of accidental contact.

I slide toward him.

"Zelda. Don't."

I stop, then draw in a breath. "Here's the thing," I say. "I don't believe in denying myself things that I want. I've had too much taken away from me. Now I fight for the things that matter to me."

His mouth tugs into a grin. "You don't know me well enough for me to matter."

"Probably not. But I can't help the way I feel. And I know you feel it, too."

"I already told you I did."

"So what's the problem? Parts not working anymore?"

He actually laughs, which is good. I thought he might be pissed off.

"Trust me. Everything works fine." I think I hear a sensual growl in his voice, but that might just be my wishful thinking. Even so, I scoot closer toward him on the sofa.

"Prove it."

"Stop it. I told you we're not going there. I'm a grownup, Zelda. Self-control comes with the package."

"Do not patronize me," I snap.

"I mean it. We're not going to get involved."

"Who said anything about involved?" I counter. "I'm talking about sex. I never get involved."

I watch as his face goes dark. "Neither do I."

There's something chilling in his tone. "What happened?"

For a moment, I don't think he's going to answer me. When he does, he's looking at the sofa cushion, not at me. "They died."

They? I almost make a crack about a threesome, then I realize he's talking about a family.

"Oh, Jasper. "You had a wife. A family."

He nods. "A little girl."

I close my eyes. "I'm so sorry."

"They're my obsession. My mission."

I run his words through my head, trying to put them in the context of this conversation. "So you're celibate?"

He laughs, and there's genuine humor in the sound. "No. Not celibate. Not by a long shot."

"Then we don't have a problem." I keep my voice teasing and bubbly in a deliberate attempt to lighten the moment. I think it works, because when he responds to me there's a hint of a smile in his voice.

"Oh, we definitely do."

"Yeah? What's that?"

He looks at me, all humor draining from his face. "Someone is threatening to kill you."

I sag, the humor and lightness going right out the window. "Right. And you really think there's meat behind that, not just some jerk being an asshole and trying to scare me."

"Honestly? I don't know." He reaches over and takes my hand, then squeezes it. "But I'm going to find out. That's why I'm here. Not sex. I'm here to keep you safe and to get answers. And Zelda, I'm going to do my job."

I nod, suddenly feeling sober. We're looking at each other, not saying anything, when my phone buzzes. "Someone's at the gate," I say, recognizing the tone.

I put it on speaker, and Frank tells us that the team from Stark Security has arrived. I authorize access, and a few minutes later, there are four members of Stark Security standing in my living room. Leah, who tells me that Ryan sent her since we're friends. Mario and Owen, neither of whom

I've met but apparently work in tech and analysis. And Trevor, who I met at the party and is another field agent like Leah and Jasper.

"Why exactly are you guys here?" I ask the group.

"We're going to do a walk-through of the property and see if there's anything that needs to be upgraded," Jasper explains. "Plus, Mario and Owen are going to get into your databases, download all of the camera footage, and hook up a direct link to our offices so we can keep an eye on your place in real time. That, and a lot more details. Do you really want the full agenda?"

"No. I trust you all to do your jobs. What do you need from me?"

"I assume the computer hard drive and other equipment are in the big house?" Mario says.

I nod.

"And do you go in there at all? Or do you just live here?" That from Owen, who, like everybody else who comes to visit, seems to be fascinated with the fact that I'm not interested in living in that monstrosity.

"I live here, but I do keep an office in the big house. There's more room for bookshelves, and I can go there to write and get away from where I live." I turn my attention to Jasper. "Do I need to move my computer in here? Or can I go there to write when I want to?"

"Do you mind staying here?" Jasper asks.

"I guess not. It's just that when you start to write, you get used to having a specific space. It can throw me off for a few days if I'm not tucked in where I'm supposed to be. Then again, I'm not on a tight deadline. But why is it important?"

"The house still gets deliveries, and you have staff living there or coming and going. You mentioned that the housekeeper, Tricia, still makes meals for you and delivers them to your studio. There must be maintenance and repair teams coming in and out, not to mention landscaping, someone to take care of the pool, and—"

"I get it. It's easy to get inside if someone's determined."

Jasper nods.

"Fine. I'll stay here." I glance at him. "I'll be more distracted when I'm trying to work, but I'll get by."

"I think wherever you work there'll be distractions. A threat like this is a big distraction."

"Probably true," I say, not bothering to add that I was thinking of him. The rest of the team probably doesn't need that tidbit of information.

"I'm assuming you need to go grab a few things?" he says.

I nod. "I need my notes for sure. A few other things."

"Okay. Why don't you and Leah go do that? I'm going to stay here and work with these guys."

Five minutes later, Leah and I are walking

across the property. "You wanna tell me what's going on between the two of you?"

I wince. I should have known she'd figure out there was something. She's known me too long, after all.

"There might have been a thing at Jamie's party."

"A thing?"

"He's hot," I say. "And I didn't even know what he did for a living then."

She twists her mouth, clearly unhappy with what's going on. "Listen. Just don't be stupid. Jasper's new to Stark Security, and I don't really know him. But from what I've heard, this guy's got issues. Someone killed his family."

"I know. He told me."

"Yeah, well, I bet he didn't tell you all of it."

"All of it?" I have no idea what she's talking about.

"If I tell you this, you better not mention it to anyone, okay? I mean it. This is a family thing."

This is Leah's serious voice. The kind I heard when Camille and I used to get in trouble. Back when I felt more a part of her family than my own.

She draws a breath. "I ran him before Ryan made the offer. Full profile, as deep as I could go."

"Okay. What did you learn?"

"He left MI6, and he's been freelance for a few years."

"So?"

"So I couldn't find anything on the jobs he took."

"So what? There were probably confidentiality terms."

"Yeah, but no. You don't understand. I'm good at what I do. He must have a secret bank account because there's not enough going into his regular one. Which begs the question of why he would need a secret one. Unless he's doing work that he doesn't want anyone to have look at."

"Again, clients with confidentiality."

"Maybe. But there are still a lot of questions."

"He was a spy. That's a paranoid breed. Maybe he just doesn't like leaving a trail. That way he avoids bad guys doing what you were trying to do."

"Maybe," she admits.

"What did Ryan say?"

"Nothing to me. I just delivered the report."

"Well, there you go. If Ryan knows and still hired him, then everything must be okay."

Leah's head tilts to the side. "Tell me you're not that naïve."

We're in the house now, crossing the palatial entryway toward the hallway under the stairs that led to my study off the kitchen. I stop in the hall and face her. "Look, just tell me what you think. You're the one who brought it up, you obviously want to tell me. What do you think is going on?"

"I think he was using freelance gigs as a cover to investigate his wife and daughter's death. Now, I think he might be using Stark Security. I think he's talented but obsessed." She crosses her arm and stares me down. "Does that sound like someone you know?"

I frown. It sounded like Martin King, my former CIA hero who has spent the last three books getting in and out of various kinds of trouble, all against the backdrop of searching for his little sister's killer.

"So what if he's a little bit like King? It's not like I knew that before I was attracted to him."

"That's not my point. You did a good job writing that character. You got into his head, and you did it right. And Martin King's a fucking powder keg."

"Yeah, but he's good in bed," I quip.

She says nothing, but there's ice in her eyes.

"Come on, Leah. Just because there are some similarities between him and my character, that doesn't mean he's actually like King. He's not going to lose his shit any moment."

"You really want to fuck a powder keg?"

I look away, as if I'm conceding the point. But I'm not. Because the truth is that even with a potential explosion, I still want him. Maybe even more.

And I'm not at all sure what that says about me.

CHAPTER NINE

After walking the perimeter with Mario, Owen, and Trevor, Jasper returned to the cottage. He saw Leah and Zelda going inside with a box from Zelda's office, so he shifted his trajectory and headed toward the main house instead.

He wanted to give Zelda her privacy. Time to catch up with Leah, and time to think about everything that was happening without him—a bodyguard, a distraction—standing in the sidelines. Plus, he needed to familiarize himself with the house in case it ever became the field of engagement. Most of all, he wanted to see the kind of environment in which Zelda had grown up.

The door was answered almost immediately. "I'm Tricia," the woman said. He guessed she was almost seventy, and she had a warm smile and a friendly but commanding manner. "Ms. Zelda asked that I show you every place in the house that you wish to see. Would you like the full tour?"

"That would be perfect," he said, not realizing just how long the tour would take. The place was palatial, with massive bedrooms, huge sitting areas, and several wings. They visited room after room filled with comfortable furniture meant for lounging, then rooms with so much crystal and silk they sparkled like a jewelry box.

Finally, he met the day staff—the workers who came in each morning to help clean, to help cook, to repair and maintain. One of their duties was delivering meals planned by Tricia to Zelda's cottage every day. But Tricia told Jasper that Zelda mostly fended for herself. "I would happily plan her three meals a day, but most weeks, she doesn't even want one. I have to beg her to accept a meal at least two evenings a week."

As far as he could tell, the woman had a motherly concern for Zelda, and he learned that she'd been working for the family since before Zelda's father had passed away.

From his talks with the staff, he realized that loyalty and discretion were highly valued. Nobody that he spoke to told him anything of substance about Zelda's deceased father or about her mother and stepfather. From the dossier Ryan sent him, Jasper knew that her father had died when Zelda was four, and her mother—Amelia—had married Carter Malloy when Zelda was seven.

Her parents had a prenup, and upon his death, Zelda had inherited everything from her father. Everything except the property was transferred to Zelda directly, making her one of the richest women in the country. As for house and land, that was put into a trust for Zelda, with the provision that her mother was allowed to live there until her death.

If Zelda pre-deceased her mother, the trust would dissolve, and the title would go to Amelia. Otherwise, the trust dissolved when Amelia passed, and the house would transfer to Zelda.

Though they had the right to live there, Amelia and Carter rarely stayed even a week. According to one magazine profile, they'd gone to Florence after their wedding, then traveled the world, leaving young Zelda at home with Tricia.

Jasper had felt ill as he'd read the article. Did these people not understand how precious it was to have a child? He would have given anything to spend long days in a house with his daughter and wife. Instead, those people had essentially abandoned Zelda, walking away without a backward glance.

Despite knowing so much about her background, Zelda herself remained an enigma, though an appealing one. A woman who'd grown up with neglectful parents who said what she thought. A woman who wasn't shy about sex but didn't want a relationship. Although with her mother and Carter as role models, he could hardly blame her.

A woman with the drive and imagination to build a career for herself out of nothing while she was still a child. Her work shifting from her early fantasy series to the much colder and darker thrillers that had made her name as an adult.

He hadn't finished *Intercontinental* yet, but he had to admit that he was entertained by the over-the-top thriller. Especially by super spy Martin King, a man who'd left government service to work on his own. Suave and deadly, King would do anything to get his man.

Jasper couldn't help but like the character.

Bottom line? Zelda Clayton was fascinating, self-confident, sexy as hell. But it was quite possible that she was trying to center herself in the middle of a huge scam. He wanted to believe her when she said that she had no such intentions. That she was insulted that the possibility even came up. But there was no denying the fact that it would be awesome publicity for the book series and for the upcoming movie if it turned out that this threat became known to the public.

All eyes would be on Zelda and her books. And Hollywood was all about the buzz.

His head and his training told him to stay vigilant, to not trust her, to watch and wait and see.

His gut and his instinct told him that she was the victim here. A talented and vibrant woman who had caught the eye of someone dangerous. A woman who needed his help.

His heart said she needed him. That he had to stay beside her. Had to protect her. That maybe, just maybe she'd be the one to help shatter the wall he'd built around himself.

And as for his cock ... well, it was possible that his trust was being driven by that particular organ. Because damned if he didn't want to be as close to the woman as he could possibly get. He wanted to bury himself in her, use her, please her.

He wanted to help her forget the nightmare spinning around her.

And, yes, he wanted to forget his own.

Fuck.

He should have had Ryan take him off the case. He wasn't clear enough. Wasn't sharp enough.

But he also knew that if Ryan tried, Jasper would put up one hell of a fight. She was his responsibility now, and damned if he was going to let anyone rip that away from him.

He cut short the rest of the house tour, his thoughts overwhelming him. He wanted to see her. To settle his impression of her. To let his instincts choose one side or another. Was she the victim, or was she behind all of this?

He headed back the cottage and found her in the living room.

She turned, eyes wide. "Oh. I thought Leah had come back."

"Sorry. It's only me."

She smiled, so wide and genuine that it felt as welcoming as a cool breeze.

"No. I'm glad to see you. I like the company, which is totally weird for me. But since this whole thing started, I don't feel safe in my own skin anymore."

His heart twisted, hating that he had no magic cure for her. "I'm sorry about that. It's not an uncommon reaction, but I am sorry."

She shrugged. "Thanks."

She was stretched out on the couch, her laptop nestled on the tray in front of her. "Are you working? Should I go into my room?"

"No. It's fine. And sorry about your room. It's tiny."

"Don't worry. I'm very adaptable."

"Well, my room's quite large, and you know there's always an open offer..."

He laughed, but his voice was firm. "I'm here to do a job, remember? And it's going to be easier if we don't tease each other about things that aren't going to happen."

"Maybe I still want them to happen."

He moved closer and leaned against the arm of the couch by her feet. "Did anyone ever tell you you're very forward?"

"Actually yes. Is that a problem?"

He couldn't help but laugh. "Not at all. So long

as you're good at managing disappointment. Some children aren't."

She stared up at him, her brows rising. "Them's fighting words." She started to pull her T-shirt up, then paused to meet his eyes. "Want me to prove just how adult I am?"

Desperately. "No. That's definitely not needed. I've read your dossier."

"Oh really?" She put her computer on the ground and pulled her knees up, freeing the cushion for him to sit. "Do tell all. I'm dying to know all about myself."

He chuckled, then sat before rattling off her biography. As he did, she stretched out again, her feet on his thighs.

"Wow, that sort of proves my point, though, don't you think? I can't possibly be only twenty-four. If I've done all that, I must be closer to thirty." She teased her foot down until her toes brushed his cock. "Wanna fuck a thirty-year-old?"

"You are incorrigible," he said, frustrated that his cock was clearly not onboard with the no-fooling-around rule.

"Is that what you call it? I usually just say horny."

He fought not to laugh. "You're saying that your age doesn't matter at all?"

She shrugged. "Well, it gets me press. Which helps get sales. So I guess that's good."

"I meant here," he admitted. "Right now."

For a moment, she looked confused. Then she bit her lower lip, giving her a sultry expression that really did make her look even older than her years. "That's what I've been saying all along. I'm not too young at all. In fact, I hope you like older women."

He cringed, realizing his mistake too late. "Whoa, slow down. I thought we'd already burned that bridge. I meant the threats. Is it a vendetta specifically based on your age? On what you've accomplished so young?"

She threw her head back and groaned, then withdrew her feet. She sat up, tucking them under her. "Fine, we'll talk work. But I'm not dropping this. You brought it back up."

"No, I didn't. I—*shit*." He drew in a breath. "Why are you pushing so hard?"

She pressed her lips together, then shrugged. "I like to get what I want."

"And I deny myself a lot of things I want," he countered. "It's partly why I'm in good enough shape to protect you. I deny myself a lot of ice cream and candy. And cheesecake. I love cheese-cake. But I don't eat a lot of it."

She rolled her eyes. "It's not like I want to marry you. I just—"

"What? You just want to prove that you're young and beautiful and can seduce anyone?" He felt his temper flaring and knew he should tamp it down. But the woman was so damned infuriating. "Well, guess what, you can. I'm right here, and I want you. Seduction achieved. But I'm going to do right by you. You're my client. I'm too old for you. And whatever this is, it isn't going anywhere."

"Fine. Whatever. Fine."

He stifled a curse and rubbed his temples. "Fine?" he repeated.

She leaned her head back and sighed. When she looked at him again, she seemed even younger. "Look, I know I'm a mess. I just—I just want the connection. And don't flatter yourself. It's not just you. I mean, I'm attracted to you, yeah. But..." She trailed off with a shrug.

"I get it. You're lonely."

"That sounds so pathetic, but it's kind of true. I never connected with anyone in college. I was too young to even drink, and it was all about frat parties and keggers."

"You're out of college now."

"Sure. And I tried to meet people. Other recent grads. I was nineteen and was already a working writer, and my fantasy life was going strong. I thought I'd find someone and we'd fall in love and it would be like a fairytale. Like I was Rapunzel and he'd rescue me from the witch and the haunted castle."

"Didn't work out as planned?"

"Nope." She stretched out again, raising her eyebrows in question and putting her feet in his lap.

He nodded consent, and she continued with

her story. "I didn't have a clue what a good relationship looked like, and I didn't know what to expect. I wanted—I wanted a connection. But everyone I met was fresh out of school, and they were focused on their career. And most of them thought I was a freak. And if it did get to the point where I brought them home, they'd either start lusting for my money or they'd freak out by what they considered some weird responsibility."

"I'm sorry," he said, realizing that he'd been rubbing her feet without even thinking about it. "Growing up is never easy, but you had it worse. You jumped straight over childhood."

She blinked, and he was surprised to see her eyes glisten with tears. "Do you know, other than Evelyn, no one has ever understood that?" Her smile was watery. "Maybe that's why I'm attracted to you. That and the fact that you're really, really hot."

He laughed.

"Honestly, I think you're just a unicorn."

"You're going to have to explain that one."

"You're older. You're smart. You're not competitive. And you don't want to get serious any more than I do."

"I don't even want—"

"I know, I know," she said. "I mean in general. The hypothetical partner. Someone to make you—me—feel wanted." She shrugged. "God, this is pathetic. I feel like I'm on a shrink's couch. But all I want is to feel. To forget. This threat, even my life. I just want to be swept away."

"That's not my job," he said, although he couldn't deny that he wanted it to be.

"I know. You've made that perfectly clear. I'm just talking. I don't even know why, except that you're listening. You are listening, aren't you?"

"I'm listening," he said. Right then, he felt like he could listen to her all night. She fascinated him, and even though he knew there was danger lurking there, he couldn't help but be drawn to her.

"But that's what it was at the party, you know. With you, I mean. I saw you at the party, and it was like being hit. And honestly, I was a little drunk— okay, a lot drunk—at that party, and when I saw you, it was just like, wow. And then in the atrium, when I realized you were attracted to me, too, I just thought it was going to happen. And then you shut it down. And now it's like someone took my cheese-cake away."

He shook his head. "Oh no. You're not allowed to try to get me to empathize by comparing sex to cheesecake."

"But you want cheesecake. You know you do."

"And I just told you that I don't have cheese-cake because it's not good for me. I can't be in good shape with cheesecake. I can't do my job as well with cheesecake."

"Fair enough. And I'm sorry if I sound like an overly chatty brat. I really do want to get to know you better. And I really do appreciate that you're protecting me."

"Thanks for that. And the truth is I want to get to know you better too. And I promise I will protect you. And just so you know, the men you've met sound like giant assholes."

"Pretty much."

"I started reading the first Martin King book." He wasn't at all sure what made him blurt that out.

"Yeah? That's totally cool. I'm being read by a guy who pretty much is King."

He chuckled. "I thought I might try and finish it tonight. See if you did it right."

Her mouth curved up in a half smile. "I always do it right. I'm the author. That means I can make up my own rules."

He couldn't help but laugh. "I bet you can. Did you write the script?"

"No. I don't know a thing about screenplays. Besides, no time. I'm already working on the next Martin King book, and I'm consulting on the series, so that takes up some time."

"The series? A Martin King TV show?"

"What? Oh, no. It's a fantasy series based on *Twisted Desire*. Have you read it?"

"No. To be honest, I hadn't even heard of it until I read the dossier on you." He watched her face, afraid he'd just insulted her. But what he saw was relief.

"Thank God. That was like everywhere when

it hit. I didn't think I'd ever be anonymous again."
She smiled up at him. "Honestly, I kind of like the
feeling. It means there's more of me for you to get to
know."

"Yeah," he said softly. "I like that part, too."

———

Jasper cupped his hands behind his head, his mind
full of Zelda.

He should be sleeping. Instead, he was remembering the delight in her eyes when he confessed to
having never heard of her first series. He could
understand wanting to be less in the spotlight.
After all, she was a celebrity. Not as much as
someone like Jamie or Damien Stark, but enough to
be inconvenienced by the steady shine of a spotlight on her life.

But to crave complete anonymity? Why?
Maybe it was just a passing thought. She was so
talented and vibrant and smart. Why didn't she
want to be out there looking at the world and see
herself reflected in it?

Just thinking about it made his heart break a
little.

But maybe it wasn't anonymity she wanted at
all. Maybe what she really wanted was to have
someone beside her. To shield her from that glare.

He felt that flutter in his chest that so often
accompanied thoughts of Zelda. Maybe he could

be the one to hold her hand. To help her feel safe in that glare.

No. Dammit, no.

He needed to exorcise those thoughts, but it was so damn hard. Because he craved her. That was the bare bones truth of it. He wanted to hold her. To possess her. To get lost with her. That vibrant, exciting woman.

He told himself it was just sex. That he wanted that release, and why not take it? So what if she was young? They both knew the attraction was real. And he was no stranger to FWB relationships.

Except he couldn't go there with her. He couldn't put his finger on why Zelda was different from Liesl or any of the women he casually fucked, but he knew that she was. He needed to stay far, far away, and not just because she was a client at his new workplace.

No, this was about protecting himself as much as it was about protecting his professional reputation.

Hell, maybe he really did need to take the edge off. As an MI6 agent, Liesl understood the way he thought and the pressure he was under even if he'd never told her his particular circumstances since he left the service. And God knew he'd relied on her enough over the years to get him by in those cold moments when he needed warmth, and Sandra wasn't there anymore.

Tonight, it was Zelda who wasn't beside him.

No, no, no.

With a groan, he let himself settle back into the thick, downy pillows. This place might be a cottage, but it was well-appointed. The pillows were fluffy, the sheets were 800 thread count, and the comforter was light as a feather. Everything was perfect, except for the fact that he was alone.

But she's only one thin wall away.

With a soft curse, he reached for his phone, intending to call Liesl. Maybe phone sex would burn this obsession right out of him. He started to dial, realized what he was doing, then tossed his phone across the room. It started to ring right as it landed.

Well, fuck. Had he actually pressed *send* instead of *cancel?*

He tossed the comforter aside, then crossed the short distance to his phone. Not Liesl, and his blood went cold when he saw the single initial identifying the contact—M.

He frowned. The initial was for Melinda Barrett. A woman he hadn't expected to ever hear from again.

She'd been his first lead. A lead it had taken years to procure. She'd been the one who'd told him about The Maestro. Who'd told her that the bookkeeper Raleigh had moved to the States, and that Raleigh might be the only person who could reveal The Maestro's identity or location.

Melinda was the reason he was at Stark Security. The reason he'd moved to the States. When he'd first found her, he'd anticipated taking her out. But in the end, he'd realized that she was as much a victim as he had been.

In a weak moment, he'd texted her his phone number and told her to reach out if she ever needed help. Or if she ever came across more information about The Maestro. So far, she was his best and only lead, and that wasn't saying much.

He connected the call, afraid to hope that maybe today was the day things changed. "Tell me you have something," he said.

"It's me," she said. "Melinda."

He closed his eyes then opened them again, calmer. "Yes. I know. Tell me you have something."

"On The Maestro? No. But Raleigh is dead."

Jasper felt his entire body go stiff. "How do you know?" Raleigh had been her boss. A bookkeeper who did work for The Maestro. And not a nice guy. He'd basically given Melinda to The Maestro for his pleasure, as if that was a perfectly acceptable form of currency.

"Someone told me."

"What? Who? Who told you what?"

"I don't know. That's the point. Someone told me that Raleigh is dead. And they said to call and tell you."

A chill ran up his spine, the kind that comes with a burst of intuition. "Was it The Maestro?"

"I don't know. I tried to recognize the voice, but he talked in a whisper. I couldn't."

"Okay. It's okay." It wasn't, but it was something. It was a lead. He wished he had more, but he would work with what he had. He tried to calm himself. To walk her through the steps. To get all the information. "Describe his voice for me."

"Like I said, he was whispering. It was raspy. He sounded older. Like my grandfather."

"What time did he call? Did he call the number that you're calling from?"

"Right before I called you, and yes."

"Okay. I want your phone. I'm going to have a friend come by and get it from you. Text me the address. We might be able to trace the location the call was made from. And right now, I want you to give me the number he called you from."

"It came in as unlisted. I don't have a number."

He closed his eyes and said a silent curse. Chances were they wouldn't be able to get anything from the phone, but he was going to try anyway. "I still want the phone. Don't worry; we'll pay you for it."

"Thank you," she said, and he knew she understood that he would be paying her well more than what the phone was worth.

"No. Thank you. I asked you to call, and you did. Now's the hard part. Tell me what he said to you. Tell me his exact words."

"I can do that," she said. "He made me write it

down." He heard her swallow, then she said, "I want you to call Jasper Kent. I want you to give him a message. Tell him the message is that Raleigh is dead and that if he wants to know more, he has to call this number."

"What number?"

"I was just getting to that. He made me write it down, too." She rattled it off, then repeated it, and he read it back to her. It was a number in the States. These days, area code didn't always match location, but with the 818 area code, there was a good chance that he was calling from the San Fernando Valley.

"You did good, Melinda. Thank you."

"Will you ever tell me why you're looking for him?"

"Probably not. But let's just say I have as much reason to hate him as you do. Maybe even more."

"That's a lot of hate."

"Yeah," he said. "It is. Goodbye, Melinda. You did good." He ended the call without waiting for her to respond. Then he drew a breath, and for the second time that night, he started to dial Liesl. This time he finished the call. She answered on the first ring. "I need a favor," he said.

"And hello to you too."

"Sorry. It's urgent." He summed up Melinda's call and gave her the address. "She's expecting you to get the phone. I want you to talk to her. See if there's anything she's not telling me. And put someone on her for the next few weeks."

"You really think she might know more about this Maestro than she's told you? She gave you this number to call."

"I don't know. But I want to find out. Mostly, though, I'm afraid she might be in danger. Why would someone call to have her forward this information? Would they really want her running around spreading this story?"

"I'll find her. I'll check on her." She paused for a moment. "Jasper?"

"What?"

"Are you going to call the number?"

He drew in a breath. Part of him wanted to walk away. To say that he didn't need this. That he was done with vendettas. That he had a good job helping good people, and he needed to move on.

But that wasn't him. He might need to move on, but he wanted answers. He couldn't move on without them. "I'm going to call. But you already knew that."

"Don't get dead on me," she said.

"Wouldn't dream of it. Thanks for checking on Melinda."

"Don't mention it. And call me if you need anything else."

"I know." That was the thing about a friend like Liesl. No matter what, he knew she would always be there for him. The thought made an image of

Zelda flash in his mind. As far as he knew, she didn't really have anybody like that. And damned if he understood why.

Once again, he looked at his phone, both wanting to make the call and dreading it.

Finally, he did it. He punched in the numbers, then pressed the button to dial, then waited for an answer.

"Yes?" The voice was low, almost a whisper. He would never recognize it if he heard the person speaking normally. His only clue was that he was almost certain the speaker was a man.

"This is Jasper Kent. I got a message to call this number."

"Kill her," the voice said. "Kill her, or others will die, too."

"Kill her? Melinda?"

"I'm hiring you, Kent," the voice said. "Kill Zelda Clayton, and in payment, I'll tell you where to find The Maestro."

CHAPTER TEN

I'm in bed, half asleep with a book on my chest when I hear the light tap at the door. The sound jerks me fully awake. At first because I'm startled—after all, usually there's no one else in this cottage with me—but also because as soon as the strangeness of the sound fades, I realize who must be doing the knocking.

"It's open."

As the door pushes inward, I slide up to a sitting position, my back against the padded head-board. I'm wearing nothing but a tank top and underwear, and I keep the sheet pulled up to my waist.

He stands there, silhouetted by the light from the living room. In contrast, my room is dark, the only illumination coming from the small clip-on light I was using to read in bed.

He's large, filling the doorway, and he looks

casual, having changed into pajama bottoms and a
plain gray T-shirt. For a moment, he just stands
there and looks at me, the inspection taking so long
that I actually pull the sheet up higher, strangely
uncomfortable.

I tug it over my breasts, then hold it in place
under my arms. Not that I was revealing anything,
but I'm suddenly feeling strangely exposed. Ironic
considering how hard I've been trying to get him in
bed since the moment I met him. He steps all the
way into the room, and I realize that one of his
hands is in his pocket. He's holding something, his
clutched hand making a bulge in the pajama
pocket.

I see his throat move as he swallows, then his
head tilts to the side, and he says, so softly that I can
barely hear him, "I'm sorry."

For a moment, cold fear rushes through me. As
if he is the one who was the danger to me all along.
"Jasper, what—"

He tugs his hand free, and I see that it's balled
into a fist. His pocket is still weighted down, but
whatever is in there, he doesn't seem to be keen on
showing me. My heart pounds in my chest, and I
curse my overactive imagination. Jasper is here to
protect me. Not hurt me.

But right now, everything seems so very, very
wrong.

He shakes his head, as if shaking off a chill, and
I hear a strange buzzing noise. It stops, then

repeats. When it starts up again, I burst out laughing, the hysterical laughter of pure relief.

It's his phone.

When he pulls it from his pocket, it's still
buzzing.

"Sorry. Just a sec." He taps out a response to
the text, then slides the phone back into his pocket,
hiding it away. Then he offers me a watery smile.
"Ryan. Sorry for the interruption."

"Why are you here?" I can't put my finger on it,
but something still seems off.

"I just wanted to tell you that everything was
calm today. No indications of any threat."

"Seriously? You came in to debrief me on
nothing?"

"Yes. No." He pinches the bridge of his nose.
"Honestly, I don't know."

"Maybe you came in to give me the chance to
apologize." I'd been looking at him, but now I
glance down as I twist my fingers in the sheet. "I've
been a brat, and I'm sorry. It's just that I like you.
But you're here on a job, and the fact that we
almost hooked up doesn't mean you owe me
anything. Not your secrets or your story. And definitely not sex, although I wouldn't turn it down." I
lift my eyes as I say the last part. "Sorry. I'm trying
to be polite and adult. I mean it. Really. Not trying
to be flip."

For a moment, he doesn't say a word. Then he
takes a step forward. "You're right. I don't owe

you. But if it makes you feel any better, I want it, too."

I bite my lip, feeling like I'm all of sixteen. "Yeah?"

"Don't be coy. You know that I do."

"But you're not going there."

"No," he says. "And yet you keep pushing. Why?"

"I'm not pushing," I say. "That's the point of this speech."

He laughs, sounding genuinely amused. I raise a brow, irritated.

"Sorry," he says. "I mean before. You pushed. And hard."

"Thus the apology. As for why...?" I trail off with a shrug. After a few moments, my chest feels tight.

"What?"

I realize I'm holding my breath. I swallow and look at my legs and torso, hidden under the sheet. At this body of mine that is craving. Wanting. "To feel," I say. "There's a sizzle with you. Electricity. I think you feel it, too, and I crave it. I really do." I draw in a breath but then rush on, afraid he'll say something before I can get it all out. "I want to feel that. I want the burn. I go out into the world, and everyone thinks that I'm so sparkly and full of sunshine, but I'm not. I'm dark and I'm alone, and I want to feel loved."

He closes his eyes, and I'm afraid I've gone too far.

"Sex isn't love."

"Maybe it's as close as I can get."

"Don't say that."

"Believe me. I wish I hadn't." I want to hit myself. I sound like I'm on a goddamn psychiatrist's couch. But there's something about this man that makes me want to share my secrets. And not just secrets, my angst. My trauma. My psychosis.

"I'm messed up," I continue. "Obviously. I put on a good show, but you came into my room to say goodnight, and I start spewing off about sleeping with you. Clearly, I'm a basket case."

"Would it help if I said that I think you're incredible?"

His words catch my attention, but his tone fills my soul. "You have very poor judgment."

"No, I don't. Say 'Thank you, Jasper.'"

I swallow. "Thank you, Jasper."

He comes and sits on the side of my bed, so close that his hip brushes my covered thigh. "What do you want, Zelda? Right now, what do you want?"

My heart pounds, my skin tingles, and my nipples are so tight he can probably see them even under the tank and the sheet.

"What I don't want is a relationship," I say, speaking rapid-fire fast. "Not that it matters, because nothing's going to happen between us, because I'm too young, and you're too old, and I'm hiring the company you work for. All of which are valid reasons even if they are stupid."

He laughs.

"What?"

"For someone who tries so hard to tell me she's not young, that sounded pretty much like a teenager."

I reach over for one of the small pillows that decorate the bed, then smack him lightly on the head. "Do you want to have a real conversation or not?"

"Not if you're going to assault me. Why don't you want a relationship?"

"Why don't you?"

His mouth curves into a grin. "I asked you first."

"Now who's acting like a teenager?"

He stares me down.

"Fine. I don't want one because they're not real. They don't last. People die or they leave." I think about Mark, my first boyfriend. I'd been twelve years old and we'd been best friends and so in love. At least, what passed for love at twelve, and I'd thought that being with him would fix everything that was bad about being in my house.

Then one day, he died. Turned out he had a defect in his heart, and he was just gone. I never trusted life again. It was too cavalier. Life had taken Mark and left me broken.

The only good thing that came out of it was *Twisted Destiny*, the series he inspired. I pumped that out of me over the course of several months of pain and loss and loneliness and do-it-yourself therapy with my fingers on a keyboard.

I'd said none of that aloud, but Jasper's looking at me like he heard it all. "Some relationships last," he says, and I snort, thinking of every failed date, every friend that moved away. And thinking of my mom and Carter, who just didn't give a crap.

"Look at Ryan and Jamie."

I shrug.

"Or Nikki and Damien Stark. They've been through hell, at least according to everything I've read in the newspapers. And they seem to be going strong. I know a lot of people with strong relationships."

"Well, aren't they the lucky ones. But that's not me."

"Maybe it could be."

"This is my reality. I have to live in it. Besides, I would think you'd approve. All the sex, none of the clinginess. It's an open offer."

"Zelda."

"Dammit, everyone's reality is different. It's spun from what we know, the world we've seen. The things we've experienced. This is mine."

"Yours sounds sad."

"And yours isn't?" I snap.

I regret the question the moment it's out of my

mouth because I can see that it's hit him with the force of a slap. His expression is a more potent answer than any he could ever speak, but when his words do come, they still break my heart.

"I loved my wife," he says, his voice low but steady. "I loved my daughter. That relationship meant everything to me, and I lost it. And I swear I will do whatever I can to find out who took them from me."

"I believe you." I want to ask him if Leah's right, and if he's been using whatever resources he can scrape together to try and track down their killer. I want to ask him if he's had any luck, and how long he's going to pursue that path. Because I can't imagine my mother lifting one single finger if I were to disappear from this earth, and the fact that he's still chasing the monster who took his family after so many years gives me a little bit of hope.

I'm just not sure that I want to have hope. It can be so disappointing if it doesn't pan out.

For a moment, nobody says anything, then he reaches over and puts his hand on my thigh. Even through the covers, I feel the heat of the connection. "You're right. Our realities are different. My daughter's life was nothing like yours. And I'm sorry for you."

I shrug. He knows my story. "But don't be sorry for me. Maybe my career is fate balancing the scales."

His brow furrows. "What do you mean?"

I shrug. "Shitty family life but good career. Maybe it's karma."

"Is that what you really think?"

I glance away. The truth is I don't have many close friends. Even outside of sex, I don't do relationships, not really. Leah's the closest, and I think that only lasted because she feels more like an aunt even though I know we somehow became friends. So yeah. I have a kick-ass career, but most of the time, I'm just lonely.

I smile up at him. "Karma really is a bitch." I put my hand over his. "But at least I'm not alone right now." I pitch my voice up at the end, like a question. Or an invitation.

For a moment we sit in silence. I don't know what he's thinking. If he's thinking about his family or my life or about my silent invitation.

As for me, I'm thinking about Karma the Bitch. If my success really is a balancing of the scales, then I'd like to take it back. Because on the whole, I think I'd rather have my dad and a better mom and no Carter Malloy at all. But my life is not one of my fantasy novels, and I can't rearrange the people in it any more than I can conjure a multiverse.

Beside me, Jasper is slowly stroking his fingertips along my forearm. The hairs are standing up, and the light tickle is more sensual than it should be. It's a caress, bare fingers against bare skin, and all I want is for it to continue.

"Jasper..." My voice trails off. I want to beg, but I also don't want to beg.

I'm not sure he even heard me, though. "You're so young," he whispers. "And so small. I could break you without the slightest effort, but all I want to do is take care of you."

"Like a pet?" I ask with a laugh.

"No," he says, without any humor in his voice. "Definitely not like a pet."

"I told you what I want," I say. "But let me remind you." I slide out from under the covers, revealing myself in just the tank and panties. "Put your back here," I say, urging him to sit where I'd been, his back against the headboard.

"Zelda."

"Just do it."

For a moment, I think he's going to say no, but then he settles onto the bed. I straddle him, feeling his erection under the thin flannel of the pajama bottoms. I rock my hips as I hold onto his shoulders so that I'm leaning forward. The tank top is very loose, the kind I usually wear with a sports bra. I know that he can see my breasts, and as I grind harder, I see him bite his lip, trying to hold back. I lean forward and brush my lips over his ear. "Admit that you like this."

"I can't really deny it." His voice is strained and only turns me on more.

"Do you want me to call you Daddy?" I whisper the tease, then feel him go tense.

"No," he says, his voice hard. "I really don't."

I lean back to see his eyes.

"That's not why I'm attracted to you."

I'd been teasing, willing to play a game. To keep everything between us about the sex. The fantasy. Because everything else gets complicated. But at the same time, I'm glad he doesn't want to play that game. "Tell me why you are attracted to me."

"No."

"No? Why not?"

"Because you don't want it to last. Which means you don't get to know. All you need to know is that I want you. Is that enough?"

My heart is pounding in my chest, and I nod. "Yes," I say.

He lifts his hands and cups my breasts. Then he raises one higher and encircles my throat. His hand is big, and he tightens it around my neck. "It would be so easy to bend you," he says. "To make you do anything I want. To break you."

"Yes," I whisper. His eyes meet mine, and we stay like that. I've stopped moving entirely, and I can feel the pressure of his hand at my throat. This could be fun. This could be dangerous.

I think about the way he looked when he walked into the room just a few minutes earlier. Like a man on a mission. A man about to destroy. Right now, I can't deny that I want him to destroy me.

He releases me, then slides me off him. I gasp in surprise.

"Get dressed. We're going out."

My whole body sags with disappointment. "I thought we shouldn't go out unless it was necessary. There might be someone watching me. And besides, don't you want to stay inside?"

"We're going out," he repeats. "And trust me. I know how to lose a tail."

CHAPTER ELEVEN

"**D**id I piss you off?" Zelda looked at him sideways at him as they walked the beach. "I mean, this was your idea, and you haven't said two words."

She was right. He was being an ass. He was the one who suggested they go out. He'd taken a circuitous route to Santa Monica, taking care to make certain they didn't have a tail, and now here they were walking barefoot in the surf under a starry sky.

It was a lovely night, and he was the one who had started this.

He was the one who was ruining it too.

"Everything's fine," he lied, the mysterious raspy voice still ringing in his head. *Kill her, and I'll tell you where to find The Maestro.*

She stopped, tilting her head as she looked up

at him. "So I didn't make you angry. This isn't about the daddy thing?"

He almost laughed, then he realized she was serious about the question. "I already told you that doesn't do it for me. But it hardly pissed me off."

"Good. It doesn't do it for me either."

"Then why'd you bring it up?"

"Hello? Because I'm trying things. I've made it perfectly clear that I want more. That I want to finish what we started. You kind of left me hanging. For that matter, you've kind of left me hanging twice now."

"So you're looking for ways to entice me into changing my mind."

"Hell, yes."

He laughed. "I'll take that under advisement."

"We get along, Jasper. You know we do. There may be two decades between us, but we get along great."

He couldn't disagree. It had been a long time since he'd felt this easy with a woman. He had a good time with Liesl, but there wasn't this kind of heat with her. That was just burning off steam. With Zelda, it felt like there might be something real.

But he wasn't sure he was ready for real.

"Did I lose you?"

He stopped walking long enough to look at her. "Just sex. That's all you want. Just sex."

"What can I say? I'm a girl who knows what

she wants. And it sounds a whole lot less complicated than getting into a relationship."

"I wouldn't be so sure," he said as he turned
around and started walking in the opposite direction. She hurried to catch up with him as he length-
ened his strides.

"Where are we going?"

"Back to the car."

"Oh. Why?"

"Because sand is itchy, and the water is cold."

For a moment, she looked confused. Then her
laughter bubbled into the night as she skipped in
the surf. "Finally."

He shook his head, laughing. Unable to deny
that this woman's exuberance was working on him.

It didn't take them long to reach his Alfa
Romeo, but he decided to drive back the long way,
and so he turned north on Sepulveda and took that
street to Mulholland, the famous dark and twisty
road that ran along the top of the hills that separated the San Fernando Valley from the West Side.

He wanted to see the night above them and
the city below, and he knew damn well he was
taking the curves too fast, but that was what this
kind of car was made for. She didn't seem to
mind at all. She held on to the handhold and
watched as the headlights cut through the dark.
And when he made a sharp left into a turnabout
with a view of the Valley, she squealed with
delight.

"You do like to live dangerously," he said, putting the car in park and killing the engine.

She shook her head. "Maybe I trust you." The words ran through him, making him want. Making him unsure what he should do. The way she made him feel reminded him of Sandra, and he didn't want to be reminded. He was afraid, he realized. Afraid that if he let Zelda in, he'd be pushing Sandra out.

Pushing her out and stopping the search for her killer.

And that had been his whole life for so long. How could he stop now?

"I would do anything to get them back, you know."

"I know," she said as if this strange segue didn't confuse her at all. "Do you want to talk about what happened?"

"No," he said. But then he began talking anyway. "They were driving. A little country road with a drop-off. Not as dangerous as this one, but there had still been accidents. From the forensic examination, we know that someone pushed them off the road. And that someone else stopped. Sandra probably thought they were trying to help. They weren't."

His voice sounded cold. Flat. Like he was presenting a paper.

"You mean they were in a turnaround on the side of the road?"

"Yes. Like this one. It had a drop-off, too. A harsh one." He looked through the windshield at the lights of the Valley below. He couldn't see how it dropped from this angle, but he knew that it did. A car could go careening over. A person could fall to their death. A spurned lover could be lost for months in the thick underbrush, battered and broken from banging on rock after rock on the way down.

It was a fall that very few could survive.

He swallowed, forcing down the memories and the anger. *Who did that? What kind of monster would do the to an innocent woman and a little girl?*

"They were killed in the fall?" Zelda's soft voice drew him back.

"No." He cleared his throat. "No, they were injured. They were killed by the man who climbed down. A man they probably assumed was trying to help."

Her hand went to her mouth, and thankfully, she didn't ask for specifics. He didn't want to think about the knife that had been used on his wife and daughter. He didn't want to remember the image of the bodies that he'd seen at the morgue, or the crime scene pictures that he demanded the police show him. He didn't want that in his head. But it was always there anyway.

"Why would someone want them dead?"

"Specifically? I don't know. Generally, I was a spy. And that's not a safe business for the people I love." He turned and looked at her directly. "That's why I don't love anymore."

She nodded slowly. "I get that." She reached over and took his hand and squeezed just a little. He expected her to say soft words, trying to ease the pain that was already etched in him, notched into his bones and flowing in his blood. Everyone wanted to try to take the edge off pain, but no one ever managed.

But that's not what she said. Instead, she said, very softly, "I could try to help you figure it out. Help you get closure."

He turned to her, his interest piqued simply from the oddity of her comment. "How on earth could you do that?"

"I don't know. But I write thrillers. I plot books. I have to think like bad guys and spies and victims. I could look over the files with you. Maybe I would see something you didn't."

He swallowed the knot in his throat. "It's a sweet offer. It truly is. I appreciate that you would even make it. But this is real life. And it's often stranger than fiction, or haven't you heard?"

"Okay," she said. "I mean, I'll buy that. But you're going to be with me for a while now. And what else are we going to do? I mean, I can think of ways to have fun, but you're old and creaky and don't seem to be interested, whereas I'm young and energetic. And I'd hate to wear you out with my enthusiasm. So I'll just stop bugging you about the whole sex thing. We can solve a mystery instead."

He laughed. "Minx."

She wrinkled her nose. "I like that word," she said, and made him laugh again. He was never this easy around anyone, and he liked that lately he kept catching himself smiling.

"So you're telling me that my choices are either endless sex with you or reverse engineering my family's death?" He managed to say the words with a note of humor. Zelda was like a tonic, and he squeezed her hand.

"Or we could just throw a party," she said. "But you're not going to let me do that because one of the guests might have gotten compromised by the bad guy, then come in and kill me in the middle of, oh, I don't know, an orgy."

"You're throwing that kind of party?"

"Well, of course. All the cool kids do."

"Hmm. Investigate a murder, have endless sex, or watch you get murdered at your own party. You do know how to give a guy some choices."

She turned toward him and smiled, all bright and sweet and innocent.

That's when it hit him.

It would be so easy. He could pull her close for a kiss, then put his hands at her throat. He could squeeze the life out of her right now, then toss her over the cliff. He could make a phone call. Take a picture of the body. He'd have his answers. He could have his answer in seconds.

He felt the pumping of his blood. That need for closure. To solve the damn riddle that had been eating him up for ten fucking years.

It would be so easy.

Except that it wouldn't be. It would be the hardest thing in the world.

He pushed open his car door. "Come on."

She got out on her side, and they met in front of the car, just feet away from the drop-off.

"It's beautiful," she said. "The lights above, the lights below."

He took her hand, then drew her to the car, urging her to sit on the hood. He stood in front of her, caging her in. "Watch the stars," he whispered. She obeyed, tilting her head back and exposing her neck.

He held her there, bending her back so that she was lying on the hood, one hand tight at her throat, then other cupping her breast through the thin material of the T-shirt she'd thrown on.

He squeezed with both hands, and she moaned, her lips parting as she closed her eyes. Christ, she was beautiful, and with his own moan that was a mix of lust and agony, he bent over her and closed his mouth over hers.

The kiss was raw and brutal, deep and claiming. He could have her, he knew. He could do

anything in that moment. Kiss her. Fuck her.
Kill her.

There was power in the knowledge, and it was
heady. But the power came from her trust, and that
was the headiest thing of all.

Slowly, he pulled back, savoring the taste of her.
She trembled in his arms, then drew in a stuttering
breath when he released his hold on her throat.

"Wow," she whispered, then swallowed. "Is
that what you're into?"

"No. Not choking or rough like that. Not
usually."

She shifted on the hood, scooting up to a sitting
position as she looked at him shyly, her teeth toying
with her lower lip. "I liked it. Surrendering. Trusting." She licked her lips. "I don't trust easily."

"Me neither," he said, then bent forward and
kissed her hard. "I like that you trust me."

She hesitated, then pulled off her shirt. She
wasn't wearing a bra, and her perfect breasts
seemed to glow in the moonlight.

"What are you doing?"

"Trusting you," she said, hitching up her skirt
as she settled back on the hood, then slid her fingers
into her panties.

His cock tightened in his jeans as he watched
her touch herself, and it was a wonder he didn't
come right then.

She opened her eyes, and he met her gaze, so

turned on it felt like he was vibrating. "Don't come," he ordered. "That's for me."

"Yes, sir," she said. "But if you don't hurry I might be naughty and disobey."

He almost laughed. Hurrying really wasn't going to be a problem. He might want to go slow, but right now, his body had other ideas.

He moved closer, and stood between her legs. Then he slid her skirt the rest of the way up, then tugged her panties down, until finally her bare ass was against the hood.

Slowly, he teased his fingers up her thighs, then dipped into her slick heat. She was so open, so ready, and so uninhibited. His finger brushed her clit and she whimpered, her body trembling against his touch.

He was as hard as steel and desperate to be inside of her. "If you're going to say no, now's the time," he said as he fumbled in his wallet for a condom.

She shook her head. "Never," she said, and he believed her. Right then, he knew with certainty that she would never deny him anything in bed. The thought was heady. Enticing. And he couldn't help but wonder how it was that he'd never felt like this with any other woman. So open. So aroused.

So damn happy.

He urged her toward him, and he teased her core with the tip of his cock, taking it slow. So deliciously, infuriatingly slow. Soon, though, he couldn't take it any longer. He withdrew long enough to turn her over, then thrust himself deep into her, his hands on her hips. She moaned, begging him for more as cars drove by their head-lights catching them each time one hit a curve.

"We can be seen," she gasped.

His breath was hot against her ear. "They're probably jealous."

"We could probably cause a traffic accident."

"In that case, baby, it's time to move this party home."

CHAPTER TWELVE

"No, no," I say, as he starts to head inside the cottage. "We're supposed to be finishing what we started."

His brows rise. "And what exactly is that?"

"Sex," I say. "You fucking me with the stars above us." I let my shoulders rise and fall. "Hey, you're the one who picked an outdoor locations. Wide open sky to get lost in. Damp night air. The feel of a breeze on bare skin."

He's fighting a laugh, but I can also tell he's intrigued. And turned on.

I step forward and cup his very hard cock. "Don't worry. Not here. No metal car hoods."

He takes my hand, lifts it to his lips, then slowly sucks on my index finger, which is, frankly, the hottest fucking thing on the planet, and I moan with pleasure. By the second finger, I've closed my eyes. When he continues to the third, I feel the draw of his mouth all the way down to my core, now throbbing and wet with need.

He stops, and I whimper. "More."

"Oh, there will be more," he assures me, then leads me to the pool deck and one of the double-wide loungers.

"I like the way you think," I say, but he presses a finger to my lip, this time to shush me.

"You don't talk. Not unless I tell you, too. Understood?"

I nod, my nipples tightening under my thin shirt.

"Undress," he says, sitting on the end of the lounger as I stand, slowly peeling all of my clothes away. I want to walk to him, then stand so close that he'd only have to lean forward to lick my clit. But that's not the way he wants to play this, and so I stay put, my body cool in the night air, my nipples tight and hard.

"Come here," he demands, and I eagerly comply. He's still seated at the end of the lounger, and as I stand in front of him, he touches me just as I'd imagined. One hand stroking lightly over my skin, the other stroking my sex, teasing my clit for the kind of slow build that is making my knees go weak.

Every once in a while, his fingers tighten on my nipple, and I feel a corresponding tug in my pussy. I want to stay like this all night, a toy for him to play with, and at the same time, I want so much more.

Then he pulls me even closer and closes his mouth over my clit as he slides two fingers inside of me. It's an overload of sensations, and I buck against him until my knees are truly too weak for me to stand, and he has to catch me as I collapse.

That's okay, though, because once I'm on the lounger, his eyes meet mine. Then he's on top of me, his body warm and perfect, with the sculpted muscles of a man with a job that relies on strength and agility.

He kisses me, long and deep, and I wrap my legs around him, silently begging for him to enter me. I want him to fill me. To use me, and when he finally does, I come almost immediately, arching up as waves of pleasure rock over me, and I hold him tight, never wanting this connection to end.

He plays it out, sending me spiraling in wave after wave of pleasure, each crest more sensational than the last. Finally, when I'm sure my body will simply evaporate, he explodes inside me, his low cry of pleasure echoing over the ten acres.

When we finally separate, I snuggle against him, happier than I've been in a very long time. "That was amazing. You're amazing."

"I think *we're* amazing," he retorts, and I really can't disagree.

And the best part? We want the same thing. Sex. Just sex.

No expectation of a commitment. Just burning

off energy and calming my nerves. I have a death threat against me, after all.

Which is all true.

But what's also true is that he's going to leave soon. Just like everyone leaves. Friends. Family.

In the end, you can only count on yourself and death. And right now, death is looming a little too close.

I shudder.

"Hey, are you okay?" Jasper runs his fingers lightly up and down my bare arm.

"Sorry. Just thinking about death."

Jasper's brows rise, then he props himself up on an elbow and stares down at me. "I didn't realize I had that effect on women. I guess I'll have to work on my technique."

Despite myself, I laugh. "Yeah. You're pretty deadly."

He reaches out and strokes my hair, tucking a lock behind my ear. It's sweet and intimate, and I want to lean into it. But I don't. "What's going on in that head of yours?"

"Just thinking about how great it is that we have the same perspective. Neither one of us wants a commitment. This is just for fun. And that's pretty great since I need fun while there's a death threat hanging over me."

I watch his eyes while I speak, looking to see if he agrees with my words. I tell myself I'm only looking for reactions. Ticks and giveaways I can use in my books. But the truth is, I want to see his reaction to my comment about commitment. I want to know if, maybe, when all this is over, he'll want to stay.

My heart does a little flip as that reality hits me. *Everyone leaves.* I know this. It's the way my life is. It's the reason I don't get close.

Yet somewhere along the way, I let myself believe that Jasper might be different. I don't know where that came from because he's certainly never given me that impression. And yet there it is, filling my thoughts, the world, my universe. *Hope.*

And so I do the only thing I can do to take my mind off the question. I straddle him, then lower my mouth to his. The kiss is long and deep, and he is all in with me. We pull apart, breathless, just long enough for our eyes to meet. "Okay?"

"Do you even have to ask?"

I grin, then slide my hand down and feel his erection. I don't answer. I just kiss him again, my tongue warring with his. And then, very slowly, I straddle him and ride him one more time until we both go supernova into the black night sky.

He's asleep when I awake the next morning, brought back to life by the stream of light coming in through the blinds and tickling my nose.

I grab my phone to check the time and see that

it's already almost ten. I stifle a groan, then slide out of bed, leaving him sleeping soundly. I have a feeling he doesn't usually laze in bed this late, but neither of us got much sleep last night.

I smile, thinking about the reason as I head into the kitchen. My plan is to grab a yogurt cup from the fridge, but somehow I find myself breaking eggs and popping toast into the toaster. It's a little bit of a miracle I have any of these things, but Tricia, bless her, keeps the fridge stocked with foods.

She knows that I'll cook if the food is in the house, otherwise I'll live on granola and string cheese. And, of course, popcorn.

I make up plates for both of us with bacon, eggs, and toast. Then I put the plates on a tray, add a bowl of strawberries and a pot of coffee, and carry it back to bed. He's just waking up, and I can see his eyes widen when I step into the room.

"To what do I owe this pleasure?" he asks.

"Let's just say that you earned it last night."

He laughs. "I'll have to work on my technique. Waffles. Quiche. The possibilities are endless."

"I look forward to your continued efforts."

I set the tray down at the foot of the bed, then climb in beside him. It's casual and easy, and we talk about nothing important as we eat. Nothing about the death threat against me, nothing about my offer to help him figure out who killed his family, nothing about the pages I have due on my upcoming book. Nothing about his work at Stark Security or before in MI6.

Instead, we talk normal things. How breakfast tastes, our favorite brunch. Mine was in New Orleans on a trip after college. A huge jazz brunch with everything imaginable. His was at a hotel in Paris, and he stuffed himself so full of cheese and bread that he thought he was going to have to be rolled back to his own hotel.

We share our favorite movies and the places we've travelled. We talk about how pretty the day is, and that leads into the question of how wonderful the night could be. "We should go out again tonight," I say with a fake leer to punctuate the comment.

He looks at me sideways. "I took a risk last night. Not only a risk of getting you killed but of getting us arrested for public indecency."

"Maybe that was the best part," I say.

"Maybe it was," he agrees. "But not tonight. We should stay in. I'm not going to risk your safety. Not again, anyway."

"So why did you take me out last night?" I ask.

"What do you mean?"

"You just decided that we should go out. It was wonderful, but you're not exactly shrug-off-the-rules guy. Was it just for me?" I move the tray aside and climb onto his lap, facing him. "Did you think I would pout if you didn't take me out?"

"Yeah," he says drily. "Something like that."

I raise a brow to stare him down. He laughs, but I keep on staring.

"It felt right," he finally says. "A walk on the beach. And then, well, I wanted the drive. I wanted you." He cups my cheek. "Is that so bad?"

"No," I say, leaning into his hand. "It's not so bad at all. Would I have suggested a repeat if it was?"

"But you're right," he continues. "It was out of character considering my job here. Tonight we stay in."

"That sounds great. If you want, we could go over everything that happened ten years ago. Like I said, we could look at it as if we were plotting a book. Martin King solves a cold case."

He bends forward and kisses my forehead. "It's sweet for you to offer, but I don't know that I want that day in my head. Not when I have you beside me. Does that make sense?"

I nod; it does make sense. But I want him to be able to talk about it with me. I want it, I realize, because that would prove that he's actually moved on. That he knows that his wife and daughter are in the past.

And I'm the one in the present.

The nature of my thoughts—of what my desire to investigate his family's murder means—comes over me like a crashing wave. I frown, then slide off the bed.

"Are you okay?"

I nod. "Yeah. Just had to stretch my legs. Maybe we should go for a walk this evening. Just around my property," I add quickly. "Get out. Fresh air."

"That's not a bad idea. But I was thinking maybe we should invite some of your friends over."

"Oh. Well, we could, but that would be a very small group of zero."

He laughs. "I think you're exaggerating. I know you're friends with Leah. I figured she'd be on the guest list."

"I'm not exaggerating that much," I tell him, my lack of social connections making me feel more than a little lame. "I told you I don't make friends easily. And when I do, they all seem to disappear."

"Zelda..."

"No, it's true. Most of the friends I've made live halfway across the country now, and I don't think they're going to fly in just for wine and cheese. Especially since we're not close anymore. I mean, Camille and I barely have a thing in common now."

I shake my head, remembering our last awkward conversation at brunch.

He starts to say something, but I cut him off. "There are some online folks I chat with while I write, but they're scattered all over the globe, and we mostly talk plots and writing schedules." I shrug. "It's not a big deal. It is what it is."

Except, of course, it is a big deal. I sigh, thinking about all the opportunities I've had over the years to make friends through local writing groups or people that Evelyn introduced me to. And there were a couple of girls at my yoga class who mentioned getting together to explore all of LA's parks.

But all those opportunities petered away because I was too scared to get invested. I don't tell him that, though. Honestly, I'm not sure I've ever told myself that before now. Something about being with Jasper Kent has made me take a closer look at myself. And I'm starting to wonder if I like what I see.

"Hey, it's no problem," he says, with the kind of cheeriness in his voice that is reserved for people who are just a little bit on the edge. He takes my hand, and I glance up at him. "We'll just drag people in off the street," he says dryly, and this time I really do laugh.

"Yeah. We'll just make sure that your random people aren't inclined to shoot me."

"I'll do a thorough investigation."

"You're going to walk, too, aren't you?" The words that have burst out of my mouth surprise me. "Once this is all over. You're gone. You won't be a friend I can call over for an evening. And you won't be the guy in my bed. Not anymore."

He looks at me like a deer caught in the head-lights. "I'll always come over. But for drinks and a movie. Or to sit around playing Trivial Pursuit. Nothing else."

"Not even friends with benefits? The benefits are pretty awesome."

He looks at me, and for a moment I don't think he's going to answer. Finally he says, "No. Not friends with benefits. Not after this is over."

"Oh," I say as a lump forms in my throat. "Well, thank you for the truth."

But as I hold that truth in my hands, I honestly don't know if it's a good thing or a bad one.

CHAPTER THIRTEEN

A quadruple threat in the entertainment industry, Matthew Holt's Hardline Entertainment dominated music, film, television, and publishing. Over the years, Holt had grown his company from a small music studio into a full-on entertainment conglomerate. Through its various divisions, the company produced bestselling novels, record-breaking and Grammy Award winning albums, Academy Award winning movies, and television series that shot to the top of everyone's Best Of lists. The Hardline streaming channel had launched less than three years ago and was already one of the most lucrative in the business.

Holt was respected and revered. A major power player in Hollywood with a reputation for brilliance in business and eyebrow-raising antics in his personal life. He wasn't a man to cross, and he could make or break a career.

And he commanded it all from his massive complex of offices, studios, and sets in Culver City. Now he leaned against a window in his fifteenth floor penthouse suite, the view of the lot that he'd bought from a defunct studio spread out behind him.

"There's very little I wouldn't do to publicize one of my movies," Holt said, his dark eyes shifting from Ryan to Jasper, both of whom were standing in front of him. He lifted the photocopy of the threat they'd shared with him and shook it. "But faking a threat to the writer is on that very short list."

He crossed his arms over his chest, his brows rising as he looked to Ryan. "We've known each other a long time now. Do you honestly think I did this?"

"What I think is that Zelda deserves the same level of protection all Stark Security clients get," Ryan said. "And if that means I piss off the man who signs my wife's paychecks, then so be it."

Holt grimaced, then moved from the window to the sitting area in his office. He sank into a deep leather chair, then indicated Ryan and Jasper should take the sofa.

"The truth is, we don't know where the threat is coming from," Jasper said, leaning back and stretching his legs. The man was intimidating as hell, and Jasper was determined to look as casual as possible.

He knew the drill. Powerful men knew how to hold their cards close to the vest. Even if Holt wasn't behind the threat—and Jasper didn't believe that he was—he might know something. Someone on his team might be overenthusiastic, and Holt might have gotten a whiff of it. It would be in his nature to cover it up to save his studio. Or he might not even realize he knew it until they started talking.

Which meant that the more casual Jasper and Ryan appeared, the more likely Holt would talk to them as friends rather than as interrogators.

Matthew's's gaze shifted from Jasper to Ryan and then back again. Then he glanced pointedly at Jasper's legs. The laid-back posture. "Should we just go get drinks?"

Jasper frowned. "Sorry?"

Matthew laughed. "You're getting all casual. Putting me at ease so I'll talk to you as friends. Not as the man who owns this studio."

Jasper cleared his throat. People said the man was sharp. They were right.

"I'll make it easy on you. I don't know the source of this threat, but I do know where it's coming from. And I can guess when it's going down."

"You son-of-a-bitch," Jasper said, his blood beginning to boil. "You think you can play with people's lives this way? What kind of strings are you pulling to promote your goddamn movie?"

He started to launch himself out of his chair, but Ryan clutched his arm and tugged him firmly back.

"Calm down," Matthew snapped. "I'm not pulling any strings. All I've done is think about what you told me. About this," he added, crumpling the photocopy of the threat and tossing it at Jasper.

"What do you mean?" Jasper's voice was tight as he tried to ratchet down his temper.

"Did you read the damn book? It'll come from a crowd. A sniper rifle. Just like in *Intercontinental*. Just like Martin King when he was walking Darby down the red carpet to the diplomatic ball."

In the book, the threat had been a hoax. But then someone else had stepped in, taking advantage after the original perp had been apprehended. A clever plot twist in which the characters believed all was well. They'd been wrong.

"The premier won't be for another year," Ryan said. "I don't get the feeling our perp is a long-term operator."

"No. Nor do I." He lifted his hand, then used two fingers to rub his forehead as if staving off a migraine. "We haven't announced it in the press yet, but Zelda will be joining Jamie at the gala opening of another one of our movies next week. A Francesca Murratti film. We're going to show a quick trailer for *Intercontinental*, then have a 2-

hour gala event celebrating both movies before screening the feature. Red carpet, full meal deal."

Ryan and Jasper exchanged looks. Zelda hadn't said a word about it. If she knew, that put her back firmly on the suspect list. A failed attack at a gala event would be one hell of a publicity stunt.

"Does Zelda know about this?" Jasper asked, and the few seconds between the question and the answer felt like hours.

"No. Everyone believes the gala is just for Frannie's new film. We're hoping for even more *Intercontinental* buzz following the surprise."

Jasper nodded, almost melting with relief.

Ryan looked at him, his brow raised. Jasper shook his head, trying to dismiss Ryan's curiosity as much as his own emotion. This wasn't good. The relief he felt wasn't simply that his client wasn't dirty. It was Zelda. The woman. *His* woman.

How the hell had he gotten in so deep with her, and how the hell was he going to dig himself out of it?

More important, did he even want to?

"Who does know?" Ryan asked.

Holt explained that the publicity department knew. Jamie knew, and so did Evelyn Dodge, who represented both Jamie and Zelda.

"All right," Jasper said, trying to get his head back in the game, "where's the overlap? Who knows about this gala and also has access to the graphic that was used in that threat?"

"Anyone could have designed that graphic," Ryan said. "It's pretty simple. Hell, they could have just photocopied the book."

"No," Holt said. "No, it's different. Good catch." He pointed at Jasper, then stood and started pacing. "This could mean something."

He stopped walking, then frowned. "I don't know what I'm getting so excited about. If it means something, it's probably coming from my publicity department."

"Explain," Jasper said.

Matthew pointed to the crumpled threat, still on the sofa by Jasper. "We went through about a billion versions of that image. We used it on the chapter headings, and we're going to be using it on all of the marketing, especially as we get closer to release. The image on that threat isn't the one that ended up in the book. It's close, but not right. Not exactly."

He stood up and crossed to the far wall of the office, lined with bookcases. He pulled down a familiar hardback, then opened it to one of the chapters. Jasper looked at the graphic, then back at the target image on the threat he'd unfolded. At first, he didn't see the difference. Then he noticed that there were a few extra circles making up the target, some lines were slightly thinner, and one was slightly blurred. "We wanted to give it a hint of motion," Holt explained.

"That does make it sound like someone in your publishing or publicity department's behind this," Ryan said. "Sorry, Matthew."

Matthew drew a breath as if collecting himself. "Yes, it does." He sighed. "But it's not for certain. Anybody on both teams would've had it. Zelda, Evelyn. Zelda's marketing team. During the decision-making process, we shared the folder with all the draft versions of the target."

"Well, that widens the field," Jasper said with a frown.

"Yes. But it hasn't been printed anywhere yet. Which means that it has to be someone who had access to the folder."

"All right. This is a line to tug on. And in the meantime, we need to be tugging fast," Ryan said. "When is this premiere?"

"Next Friday," Holt said. "But as I mentioned, the *Intercontinental* trailer is a surprise. The guests believe they're coming only to a premier and a party. We're not advertising the *Intercontinental* connection."

"But people who worked on the film or marketing know," Ryan said, and Matthew nodded.

"That's got to be where it's going to happen," Jasper said.

He wanted to kick himself. Granted, he hadn't known about this gala. But she'd written a damn book, and there was a movie attached to it. That meant events. Even small publicity appearances. More book signings.

But did that threat even really exist? Was it just a false lead, directing them away from the one who was supposed to kill her? Directing them away from *him*.

What if there was no man with a gun? No assassin coming to the premiere? What if this was just the setup of a wild goose chase?

Because the perp they were truly looking for wasn't a sniper at a gala. Instead, it was the puppet master who was pulling strings, trying to get Jasper to pull the trigger.

And that person was going to be a lot harder to find.

But no, his puppet master was smart. He'd have a backup plan. And when he realized that Jasper wasn't going to take out Zelda, he'd put that plan in place.

There *would* be someone at that gala with a weapon. A knife. A sniper rifle. Maybe even poison.

Someone who would take Zelda out, stealing her from him.

And at the same time destroying every chance Jasper had to find out who killed Sandra and Bonnie.

Jasper returned from the meeting with Matthew Holt to find Leah pacing in front of the cottage and fuming.

"What the hell are you doing?" he asked. "You're supposed to be with Zelda."

She stopped, her eyes slamming against his, fury burning under the surface. "I've got eyes on," she snapped, then nodded to a table by the massive pool and deck that separated the cottage from the house. "But I was told to stay at a distance."

Her voice was hard. Angry. And he let his own fury subside. She was pissed off enough for the both of them.

"Who the hell are they?" he asked.

He knew Leah well enough to know that she wouldn't have left Zelda alone with a threat. Still, he didn't like the fact that there wasn't someone from the SSA team right at her side.

"Her parents."

"And you left her alone with them?"

Her brow rose. "Do you really think they're going to blow her away? Poison her?"

He didn't. But he also hated them on principle. "I wouldn't put anything past them."

Leah stared him down. "Can't argue with that. But I doubt they'll drown her in the swimming pool."

"No," he conceded. "Christ, but she can't stand them."

"I didn't realize you knew how fraught their relationship is." She gave him a hard look as if she'd seen more on his face than he wanted her to.

"Of course, I know. I've been staying with her. Guarding her. We talk. Conversation is a thing. And she told me a bit about the way she grew up. It sucked."

"Yeah. I know. I've known her since she was a kid. My niece was her best friend until my aunt and uncle packed up and moved the family to Ohio."

"So is her relationship with Mommy and Daddy dearest as bad as I get the impression it is?"

"From what I've seen, yeah. But then again, a lot of kids have terrible relationships with their parents."

He glanced back over to where she sat stiff in the chair across from her mother and Carter Malloy. "She should have someone with her."

"She told me it was fine. They wanted to talk to her alone, and she said it was okay."

"For you maybe. Not for me. Do they know why you're here?"

"You mean the threat? No. They don't know a thing about that. They think I was just visiting."

"All right. I'm going to go over there. She can get pissed at me if she wants to, but I'm staying by her side. What?" he asked when he saw Leah's mouth curve up.

"Nothing," she said a bit too innocently. "Nothing at all."

He shot her a frown, then walked the stone pathway to the pool. He crossed the decking, ignoring the glare from Carter Malloy as he moved to stand behind her. He put his hands on her shoulders and bent over to kiss her hair. It felt right. It felt natural. But the truth was, it was all an act.

"Who the hell are you?" Carter asked.

Jasper caught the scent of cigars. There was no ashtray on the table, but he saw Tricia coming from the house holding one. Apparently, she had just changed it out. He wondered how long they'd been there that the ashtray needed to be removed and cleaned.

"Sorry I was late, baby," he said, then looked at her parents. "I'm Jasper. Her boyfriend."

Carter snorted. "Looking for a sugar daddy to keep you?" His tone was joking. Except that it wasn't. "You already have all the money that should be mine—and your mother's. I would've thought that would be enough."

Beneath his hands, she felt him stiffen. "You live in the house. I live in the cottage. Other than that, we really don't need to talk to each other."

"Do not talk to your father that way," her mother snapped.

"He's not my—"

"What do you want?" Jasper asked, the question directed at Carter.

The older man eyed him. "And what is it that you do, Jasper?"

Jasper chuckled, then made a show of pulling out the chair beside Zelda and stretching his legs out. "As little as possible."

Carter's eyes narrowed. "Bullshit. You're a glorified security guard. I work for a living, boy. I have power. I have resources you couldn't possibly imagine. I know who you are. I know you're here because someone is threatening our little girl."

"I am not your little girl," Zelda snapped.

"We're canceling our trip," Carter said. "I need to hop over to France, but I'll be back soon. And your mother will stay here. Right by your side."

Beside him, Zelda's mother started to open her mouth. Carter reached over and patted her hand. "You're staying," he said. "And I won't be gone long."

"Oh Christ," Zelda said. "Seriously?"

"Of course. Do you think we'd stay away when you're in danger?"

Zelda twisted up to look at him. From the look on her face, she definitely thought that.

"Listen to your father, sweetie pie," her mother said. "Security is his business. You're safer this way."

"Why on earth will I be safer?"

Her mother's mouth opened, and she gaped for a moment, like a fish drawing for air. But she didn't say anything. Apparently, Zelda had gone off script.

"And why do you even care?" Zelda continued. "Or do you figure that whoever is after me is going to manage to take me out? And if you're already here it's going to make it easier for you to do the paperwork to transfer the title to you?"

Without warning, her mother's arm lashed out, and she slapped Zelda hard across the face.

Zelda lurched back her eyes wide. "You have been a spoiled little brat your entire life. How dare you say something like that to me."

Zelda stared. Then she shoved her chair back, stood, and ran off the pool deck. Jasper shot her parents the kind of look that in a better world would have the power to render them both to dust. Then he turned and hurried after her.

"Do you want to talk about it?" he asked when he found her at the side of the cottage, sitting on a little bench by a flower garden. Tears streamed down her cheeks, and his heart broke a little. She shouldn't be crying about what either of those people thought. They weren't worth the time of day.

She shook her head "No talking."

He sat beside her and put his hand on her knee. "It's okay. I'll just sit with you. It's fine. It's all going to be fine."

"It's never been fine." She looked at him, her

eyes wide and deep. "Would you kiss me? Would you kiss me until it all goes away?"

The heart that he'd been managing to hold together with tape and glue shattered in his chest. "Oh, baby," he said, pulling her close. "I'll give you whatever you need."

CHAPTER FOURTEEN

Morning comes along with a delicious wake-up call of kisses and sex, and once Jasper has thoroughly used my body, I roll over, cuddling close. "Mmm," I say, with the same kind of satisfaction as if I'd just eaten a completely rich piece of chocolate cake. "Can't we just stay here?"

"We could," Jasper says. "But it might be awkward."

I prop myself up on an elbow. "Awkward?"

"We have company coming at six."

I glance at the clock, see that it's five-fifteen, and bolt all the way up, the sheet falling down to leave me half-naked in the bed. "What are you talking about?"

He reaches out and strokes my nipple. "Never mind. I'm thinking I might cancel."

I laugh and smack his hand away. "I'm serious.

What are you talking about?" Something like horror washes over me. "Oh no, you didn't."

He frowns. "What are you talking about?"

"You didn't invite my mother over, did you? You're not under some absurd delusion that there's hope for our relationship?"

He shakes his head. "Absolutely not."

The fact that he's so adamant calms me. Most people would have hemmed and hawed. Even if they hadn't invited her over, they would make some speech about how I should try to reconcile with my mother. The fact that Jasper didn't do that is even more proof that he's perfect for me.

Perfect for me....

I suck in air, unable to believe I really just thought that because I don't want to want to fall for this guy. Not like that. Not really.

My panicked heart pounds in my chest. Yes, I love being with him. Hanging out with him. But that's all I can handle right now. That's all I can ever handle.

I can't get invested, because I know it's going to be over. It always ends. It has to end. That's the way the world goes. Things happen, then they end.

I draw a deep breath, trying to calm down. *Perfect for me.*

Such beautiful words. But so damn terrifying.

I look up to see him staring back at me, his forehead creased with confusion.

"What's going on in that mind of yours?"

I shake my head. "I'm okay. I'm fine. I just ... it's just that you get me."

His eyes widen. "That's a bad thing?"

I scowl. "Do we get to stay all day in bed or not? If it's not my mother, then who is it?"

"Friends," he says.

"You invited friends over?" I study his face to see if this is a joke. Apparently, it's not. "Your friends?"

"Our friends."

I start to argue that we don't have mutual friends, but instead I ask, "Who? And why? Are we just going to sit around drinking and talking?"

It sounded like an awful lot of pressure to me.

Then again, I'm an expert at putting on a bright and bubbly personality. I suppose if I can do it at big events, I can do it at small ones too.

"Jamie's coming, and she said she's bringing Ollie, and Leah's coming, and she said she's going to bring someone else from Stark Security, although she didn't know who would be available, but she doesn't want to drive by herself. I invited Evelyn, but she's out of town for a few days."

"That's it?" I ask. "No one else is coming?"

He laughs. "You're complaining? Two seconds ago, you were upset that I invited anyone. I was trying to find the perfect balance."

I move closer to him, then rise up to give him a kiss. "You're right. It's the perfect number. Thank you. But why exactly are they coming?"

"To drink and chat and have fun. If you're worried we won't have anything to talk about, we'll pull out Pictionary. Or Trivial Pursuit. Maybe rely on charades. That's always a crowd pleaser."

"I think I'll rely on the drinking part," I say, making him laugh.

I climb out of bed and hold out my hand. "If they're about to descend, we should get dressed. I want to shower. Am I showering alone, or will I have company?"

I can tell by the look on his face that I'll have company. I grin, feeling happier than I can remember feeling in a long time.

"Don't even think about it," I say. "Quick shower. If we don't want them walking in on us in bed, we definitely don't want them walking in on the shower. And because you didn't give me any warning, I need to clean the place up."

"This place is tiny. And you have no things. How long could it possibly take to clean up?"

"Keep teasing me, and I'll keep you out of the shower."

He laughs and makes a motion like he's locking his lips. He reaches to grab me, and I skip happily out of the way, then lead him to the shower.

He's a little handsy when we're both soaped up, totally breaking my rules. But we manage to get clean and out of the shower in less than ten minutes. By the time Frank calls from the gatehouse to authorize Ollie's arrival into the subdivision, the house is clean, and I've even put out some snack food, thanks to an emergency call to Tricia, who whipped together a few trays for this little shindig.

Jasper checks the control panel, then opens the gate for Ollie's car. I hurry outside to greet him and Jamie, surprised when Ollie gets out with Trevor, who I met briefly when the team came to check out my security.

"Good to see you again," I tell him, even as I pull Ollie into a hug. I haven't known him for long, but he's one of Jamie's best friends. Since we met after *Intercontinental* was optioned, she and I have had lunch a few times to talk about the characters and the screenplay, and Ollie tagged along once or twice.

"Is Jamie in a different car?"

"She couldn't come. Some sort of work crisis. I asked Trevor to come with me. He'd called to see if I wanted to grab a movie—instead, I'm bringing him here."

Trevor grins. "I'm the new Jamie."

I laugh and tell him he'll do just fine. "Just be loud and have no filter," I say, and Ollie and I laugh.

The three of us go in together, and I point them toward the wine and the liquor. "Help yourself," I say.

While Trevor is filling his plate with cheese

and snacks, Ollie corners Jasper. I notice, and sidle over to join their conversation.

"Do you have any leads?" Ollie asks him.

"Are you talking about me or something else?"

"You," Jasper says. "Right now, you're the only thing I'm worried about."

He turns his attention back to Ollie and shakes his head. "Nothing. But also no new threats. We have a possible idea about where the threat might have come from, though," he says, then gives Ollie the quick and dirty rundown of the discussion he had with Matthew Holt earlier.

Ollie nods. "I know Matthew." He looks between the two of us. "If you want me to, I can follow up. Also, I can take a look at the site, check out the surroundings, see where someone might set up a sniper. Pull files and see if anyone has ever been in that situation before. See if there's any chatter about someone trying to hire a sniper."

"I'd appreciate it," Jasper says. "We've already got the SSA on it, of course, but I'm happy to have all hands on deck."

Ollie nods. "I'll coordinate with Ryan to make sure we don't waste time doing the same work. But I may have resources he doesn't have. Although, to be honest, I'm always impressed by how many resources Stark and Hunter have managed to line up for the agency."

"Do you work for the SSA?" I ask him. It's not a

question that's ever occurred to me before. All I know is that he's a former lawyer turned FBI agent.

Ollie shakes his head. "No, but we worked together on projects. And Ryan and I go way back." He looks at the two of us. "I'll let you know if I find anything out."

"Part of me doesn't want to go to that gala," I tell Jasper when we're alone. He reaches for my hand and squeezes it.

"That's totally your prerogative. The world won't fall apart if you're not at a screening."

"I know. I just don't like the idea of them winning."

"First, we don't know that the threat is actually real." He frowns, and I see a shadow cross his face.

"What?"

He shakes his head. "Nothing. That's probably just wishful thinking. We have to assume that it's real. And I hate to think of you in danger like that."

"Me too. Thus the maybe not going."

"I know." He squeezes my hand. "We're going to catch whoever's doing this, but it may take more than a week. The idea of you changing your entire life around just makes me sad. That gala is supposed to be fun for you."

"A bullet in my head doesn't sound very fun."

He squeezes my hand. "Don't think like that. I'm not losing you, too."

I think about Sandra and Bonnie, then lean

forward and brush a kiss across his cheek. "I'm pretty hard to get rid of," I say. "I promise."

He offers me a smile, and I think he's going to say something else, but then the door opens, and Leah walks in with someone I haven't yet met.

"I need to talk to Frank. She shouldn't be able to—"

"Hold on, Sheriff," I say as Leah and her companion head our way. "Leah's authorized into the subdivision, and she has the code for our property gate."

I give her a hug, then shake hands with the seriously built blond-haired, green-eyed man standing beside her.

"This is Simon. He signed on not long before Jasper. He's a little weird, but he's okay."

"Thanks a lot," Simon says as Jasper reaches out to shake his hand.

"Glad you made it," Jasper says, and I realize I'm smiling, enjoying the fact that he's playing the host with me.

"I appreciate the invite. And great to meet you, Zelda," Simon adds to me.

"He doesn't seem weird at all," I say to Leah.

"Oh, he is. He doesn't like Hollywood." She says it in a low voice, as if that's the most shocking thing in the world.

"Sounds perfectly sane and reasonable to me," I tell Simon.

"At last, someone in this town with a rational view of the world."

"Of course, you're going to suck when we play charades," I point out.

"Undoubtedly," he says, and we all laugh, then head over to where Ollie and Trevor are chatting by the makeshift bar. A drink, I think, sounds like a dandy idea.

As it turns out, I don't need alcohol to turn on Bubbly and Perky Social Zelda. On the contrary, I'm surprised by how much fun I end up having with the six of us simply sitting around talking.

At one point, the gala comes up. Simon's advice is to not go. "Not because of the danger," he says. "But because it's just Hollywood bullshit."

Leah and Trevor get into a heated discussion about whether it makes more sense to go and try to smoke out the killer or to stay in and hide. Ollie swears that he's withholding judgment since he's not offi-cially on the case and doesn't have a stake in this game.

I groan and fall backwards, leaning against Jasper, who wraps his arms around me. Leah notices and smiles.

"Can we please not discuss my impending demise right now?" I beg. "I'd like fun. More help-ings of fun."

Honestly, though, I'm not sure there could be more helpings of fun. I'm having such a good time that I think we have all the fun right here in this room already. I'm bubbly to the brim, but not because I'm putting on an act for the public. I'm genuinely enjoying myself. And the only downside is that I know this feeling will inevitably end.

We actually do play charades, and Ollie and Trevor kill it as a team, practically reading each others' minds. The biggest surprise is how well Simon does when someone picks a movie. "I said I didn't like Hollywood. I didn't say I was clueless. Frankly, I know a hell of a lot more than I want to."

Jasper and I exchange glances, and I'm sure both of us are wondering what his story is. "Do you have a clue?" I ask Jasper, but he just shakes his head. "Haven't been there long enough. But I'll find out," he assures me, and that little promise— about something unrelated to me that may take weeks to parse out— somehow means everything. Because it means that he's looking toward the future. And in the future he sees, I'm there with him.

I wait for the panic, but it doesn't come, and when he reaches for my hand, I take it, then smile happily at him.

"What?"

"Just having a good time." I rise up to kiss him. "Thanks for this," I say as he pulls me even closer.

As everyone's drifting from the game to go get more snacks and drinks, Leah pulls the two of us aside. "You guys look really good together," she says. "I was worried at first."

"Worried? How did you even know there was a thing?"

Leah just tilts her head to the side. "Seriously? I've known you forever. Plus, Tricia likes me," she says with a wink. "And I can get gossip out of anyone. And don't you dare chew her out."

I roll my eyes. She knows Tricia's the closest thing I have to real family. Of course, I'm not going to chew her out.

"I admit I was a little worried about the age thing," Leah continues. "But I'm not anymore. Not after watching you guys together tonight."

"Good," Jasper says, putting his hands on my shoulders. "The truth is Zelda's a lot older than her years. And when I'm with her, I feel a lot younger than mine."

"Oh, you've always been immature," Leah says with a wink. And on that zinger, she heads back to the bar.

"I'm having a really good time," I tell Jasper at one point when we're alone in the kitchen together.

"You should do this more often," he says.

"Those people are all your work buddies," I say.

"And they're your friends. Or they could be."

I shrug.

"People leave," he says, gently putting his hands on my shoulders. "Your dad left because he was taken by death. Your mother because she's an idiot, and your vile stepfather pulled her away."

"You think I don't know that?"

"I think you drew the short straw. And I know you believe you're cursed. That you lose the people who should be the closest to you. Mark and Camille. Your parents. Others you haven't told me about. You've tried so hard to protect yourself from that that I think you see people leaving even before they're fully in the door."

My heart twists with his words, and he continues, "Maybe you and Camille did grow apart. It happens. But you're so focused on that, you don't even see that Camille leaving opened the door to Leah, and she really is your friend."

"She thinks of me like a niece."

"Maybe at first. Not anymore. All you have to do is look out into the living room, and you'll see a room full of friends, including Leah. You just need to open the door, baby. Just let them in. I think you'll be surprised how many stay."

I stare at him, tears in my eyes.

He gently brushes one away. "I'm sorry, but—"

"No. You're right." I swallow. "I've known you for like five minutes, and you know me better than anybody. How is that even possible?"

"I don't know," he says. But in my head, I hear my own answer to the question: *Because I love you.*

He pulls me close and kisses my forehead. Then he takes a step toward the living area.

I grab his hand, making him stay. "About people leaving," I say. "Sometimes they don't go.

Sometimes they're taken. And that can feel like a door getting shut. But that doesn't mean you need to close all the windows, too."

His eyes narrow as he studies me. "What are you talking about?"

"They didn't want to leave you. Sandra and Bonnie. They didn't move away. They didn't become tired of you. You didn't grow apart. They didn't want to leave you."

I squeeze his hand. "They were taken. Neither one of them died a natural death. They didn't want to go."

My voice catches, and I wipe a tear from my cheek but continue, my throat thick. "And I'm guessing that Sandra wouldn't want you to be alone. I'm not saying you have to be with me," I add, although the thought of having him with me always feels like Christmas morning, "but just think about it what I'm saying. I'm alone because my family walked away, and it messed me up. Yours were taken, and that messed you up too. But at the end of the day," I say, looking at him through a shimmer of tears, "aren't we both punishing ourselves?"

CHAPTER FIFTEEN

J asper walked across the gravel-covered turnaround, then sat down at the edge, his feet dangling off into the void. He kicked, and his heels against the rocks sent bits of shale skittering down into the abyss below.

He was looking straight forward, not down. But he knew what was below him. Small trees growing horizontally out of the cliffside. Birds' nests. Bugs. A raw, vertical surface full of jutting rocks of different colors.

At the bottom, there were tangled trees and vines. Years of untrimmed undergrowth. And one battered blue Toyota, its tires in the air, one door ripped completely off.

He drew a breath, gathering courage, then tilted his head so he could look down into the canyon at the metal undercarriage of the car.

Clouds moved across the sky, blocking then

*revealing the sun, which reflected off the metal of the
car. A message, he thought, and he stared at the
flashes, trying to make sense of them.*

Dot. Dot. Dot.

Dash. Dash. Dash.

Dot. Dot. Dot.

The signal repeated itself over and over.

Dot. Dot. Dot.

Dash. Dash. Dash.

Dot. Dot. Dot.

*A distress call. An emergency. And here he was,
safe on solid ground. That wasn't right. He needed
to help. Carefully, he scrambled to his feet, almost
slipping once. His chest tightened. Fear engulfed
him. Adrenaline threw him back. He exhaled
sharply, realizing he could have fallen over the side.*

If he had, he would be dead.

He looked down at the car once again.

Dot. Dot. Dot.

Dash. Dash. Dash.

Dot. Dot. Dot.

*He had to help, but he didn't know how. He
looked around, for the first time noticing a knotted
rope tossed over the side of cliff. He moved to it. It
was close by, just one or two steps away. He bent
over and tugged on it. He couldn't see what it was
attached to, but it seemed secure. Carefully, he held
on just above one of the knots, then—moving hand
under hand—he slowly descended into the gorge.*

It had seemed so far down when he looked, but

he reached the car without even noticing his descent. He was suddenly just there, standing on the under-carriage.

The sun was behind a cloud now, the emergency call no longer crying out to him. Everything was still. There was no wind, no sounds from animals. No noise from cars driving on the road so far above them. It was eerie, and he felt so alone.

Then he heard it. A small sound. A mewl. Like a small cat trapped in a cupboard. He looked around, but he saw nothing.

Then he heard a faint scratching. It seemed to rise up from underneath his feet. From the car's interior. He tried to listen. Tried to figure out what the sound was. But he had no clue. It was too faint.

"Jasper!"

He froze, his head cocked. But the sound wasn't coming from the car. It was coming from above him. He looked up and saw her standing at the edge of the cliff. Immediately, fear filled him. He threw up a hand, crying for her to stop, afraid that she would fall.

"Zelda! Zelda, what are you doing?"

"I'm waiting for you. Are you coming back up?"

"I can't. Not yet." He wanted to. He wanted to climb back up that rope and hold her in his arms more than anything in the world. But he was here now for a reason. He wished he could remember why. Something about the car and the cliff and a knife.

"I have to do something," he called up to her.

"I'll help you. Let me come down to you."

The fear touched him again. "No," he shouted. "You have to stay. I can't protect you if you leave the road."

"But I want to help. They need my help too. They need me to help you."

He shook his head, the words not making sense. Who were they? And how were they supposed to help him?

He looked up at her, silently begging for more information, but she just laughed and danced along the edge, kicking small stones over the edge of the cliff. He screamed, telling her to stop, begging her to be careful. But the words never managed to leave his throat.

"Help. Daddy. Daddy, help us."

Bonnie!

He glanced at Zelda once more. She was there, dancing on that treacherous edge, but for now, she was safe.

He relaxed enough to lie on his stomach and hang his head over the side of the car. He looked in through the gap where the door used to be. Bonnie and Sandra were hanging upside down in their seats, still strapped in.

"Are you going away now?" Sandra asked.

"No. Of course not. I'm going to get you out of here."

"You don't need to," she said, then turned her neck. "It won't matter."

He saw the gaping wound, the blood dripping from her.

"No. No. I can save you."

"Daddy? Daddy, I don't want to go away." He reached out his hand, trying to touch hers, but their fingers were too many inches apart.

"I don't want you to go either. I'm going to save you."

"This isn't the way to do it," Sandra said.

"I can't abandon you."

"You'll never abandon us."

"Never," he promised.

"Even if you move on, you'll still be with us."

"I'm not moving on," he said.

"Aren't you?" She tilted her head, turning her neck so she was looking up, as if through the undercarriage of the car.

"I think you are. I think you should."

He felt the tears in his eyes, saw them fall from his eyes and past the car to land on the trees below, each tear setting off an explosion of silver sparkles. "I can't abandon you."

"You didn't. You would never. And we will always love you."

Beneath him, something cracked, and the car shifted violently. "You need to go," Sandra said. She passed the knotted rope to Bonnie. Bonnie passed it to him. He frowned at it, unsure how it had ended up in the car. He took it from his daughter's hand, looking into those big brown eyes.

"Hold on tight, Daddy."

"I can't. You can't."

"It's time," Sandra said, flashing him her sweet smile. "But don't forget. Don't forget us."

"Never. I'll never forget you, and I'll never stop searching for who did this to you."

"They hide in plain sight, you know," Sandra said. "We never saw it coming. You never saw it coming. But Jasper, my love, hindsight is twenty-twenty. All you have to do is look in the right place."

He shook his head, unable to understand the words. "What do you mean? What are you talking about?"

"Remember, look in the right place. They hide in plain sight. You would never see it coming. Good is bad and bad is good and we don't know the difference until we know. And, my love, now it's time for us to go."

"No," he began, but he didn't get to finish the sentence. Instead the word transformed into a scream as the car fell away from beneath him.

He clung to the rope, his hands tight on the knots, his feet clambering for purchase. It was shaking, the ground beneath him rumbling. He looked down, trying to see where the car had landed. But it was gone.

For a moment, the clouds shifted, revealing the

sun. He saw one flash of light below, as quick as a wink, then that was gone too.

For an eternity, he hung in the void alone.

Then he looked up. He saw Zelda.

And Jasper began to climb.

Jasper woke with a start, his cheeks wet with tears. He was groggy. Disoriented.

Then he looked down and saw the woman in his arms, and a sense of calm came over him. He was where he was supposed to be, and he had the blessing of his wife and daughter.

For the first time in a long time, life was good.

He bent over, gently kissing Zelda's bare shoulder. He knew it was just a dream, but it had soothed him. It had been a push. Hell, it had been an order. His subconscious telling him to forgive himself.

He would never stop trying to find their killer, but it was time to move on. And he knew without a shadow of a doubt that Sandra would not only want him to, but that she would adore Zelda as much as he did.

As if awakened by his thoughts, Zelda turned in his arms and smiled at him. "Hey there," she whispered, and he answered her with a kiss.

"I could get used to waking up like this."

He reached downward and gently pushed the

hair off her face, tucking it behind her ear. "I'm never going to stop looking for the monster who killed Sandra and Bonnie."

Her brow furrowed. "I know. Did something happen?"

"I had a dream about them," he told her. "Are you okay with that? Knowing that I'm not going to stop looking."

The crease between her eyebrows deepened, and she pushed herself up on an elbow. "Well, yeah. Of course. But I don't really have a say in that."

"Yeah, you do."

"I do?" She bit her lower lip, like a kid working their way through a math test. "Why?"

He took a breath. "Because I'm falling in love with you," he said, the words feeling perfect because they were real. "I know it's fast, but it's true."

He watched her eyes go wide.

"Oh."

For a moment, she said nothing, and fear started to prickle at his skin. Then her lips curved up. "Well, that's pretty convenient," she said. "Because I'm falling in love with you too."

For a moment, they simply looked at each other. Then he kissed her. He didn't intend to start something, but with Zelda, he never seemed to have any self-control. Before he knew it, he was deep inside her, passion growing as they claimed each other, each unable to get enough, until finally they exploded together in a symphony of light and pleasure.

"I think I like waking up like this," she said, then snuggled closer. Her face was buried in his neck and he could feel her breath along with the movement of her lips as she spoke. "Will you let me do something for you?" she asked.

"Anything."

She shifted, leaning back so that she was looking at him directly. "I love you. I love you, and because I do, I want you to figure it out. I want you to know who took Bonnie and Sandra away from you. Please let me help you try to figure it out. I told you I thought I could. And I meant it. I know you think it's silly, but I might see something you don't."

He stroked her hair then rubbed the pad of his thumb along her lower lip. "Are you sure? I don't want their shadows in our relationship."

"But of course they're in our life. They were your life. Where else would they be? And you deserve answers. So do they."

He didn't think it would do any good. After all, he'd been working the case for a decade. And at the same time, he never wanted to let this woman go. And if walking this path beside him was what she wanted to do, then he would accept that. Because there was no way he was going to give up. He'd meant what he said. Sandra and Bonnie deserved to be free too. And it filled his heart with joy to know that Zelda felt the same way.

"All right," he said. "We'll work this together. We'll figure it out." He rolled over and started to get out of bed. She tugged him back.

"Hold on there. Where do you think you're going?"

"I thought I might grab a shower."

"Slacker. Let's think about this."

"We don't have to right now."

"Yes we do. You had a dream." She grabbed her phone. "You need to tell me about it before you forget. And I'm going to record it."

He did, telling her as much as he could, but it was hard. The bits and pieces kept disappearing the way they do when dreams turn to smoke.

"Run it through for me again. You might remember more."

And so he told her once again.

"Hiding in plain sight," Zelda said. "Never seeing it coming and looking in the right place. Does that mean anything to you?"

He shook his head. "No. Nothing."

"Sounds to me like your subconscious thinks that you already know the answer. I mean, hiding in plain sight seems pretty definitive."

"Well, then my subconscious is a filthy bastard because it's not telling me a thing." He squeezed her hand. "I know you want to help. But we should probably move on. I don't think interpreting dreams is the kind of thing that happens when you force it. It'll probably come to me in the shower."

She wiggled her brows. "Well, showers are something I can definitely be talked into."

"Something we agree on."

He slid out of bed and held out his hand to her. She took it but stayed on the mattress as she asked, "What about motive?"

"I've thought about that for years. I have no idea. Other than me, I don't know what it could be."

"What were you working on at the time?"

"That's the thing. You'd think it would be related to my work. But I'd taken three months of leave. I'd been injured, and it was summer. Bonnie was going to be starting first grade, and we wanted to spend time. They were killed at the end of the summer. Right before school started. You'd think that anybody who'd been pissed off at me on my last case would've attacked a little bit earlier."

"But maybe not. What was the last case?"

He could tell that she was determined, which meant that he wasn't getting his sexy, soapy shower any time soon.

"If we're not showering, we're eating. I need food to think." He let go of her hand long enough to grab her robe and toss it to her.

"Fine. You cook. I'll make notes."

Moments later, she was in her fluffy robe and settled at the dining table. He was cracking eggs as he rattled off the cases that he'd worked immediately prior to that horrible summer. He'd been over this so many times he could do it from memory. There were a half dozen matters, and not a single one of them seemed like a good probability. Something he'd ruled out years ago, and which, by the end of breakfast, she'd ruled out as well.

"I warned you. You wanted in on this mystery. And it is one."

"So if it wasn't related to one of your cases, it had to be personal. You must have enemies. From earlier cases. A longtime vendetta and someone saw an opportunity. Like somebody who held a grudge after you cut them off in a parking lot, assuming that's a metaphor for something a hell of a lot bigger."

"I have enemies, yes. It comes with the whole MI6 thing. But you do know that we're not going to solve the mystery this morning. Right?"

She scowled. "I know. I just..."

"What?" he said.

"I just want this for you."

His heart melted a little. "I know," he said. "And for that, I love you desperately."

CHAPTER SIXTEEN

While Jasper spends the rest of the morning on the phone following up various leads relating to the threat against me, I go outside to catch some sun by the pool. My Fun in the Sun Day was his idea, and although I protested at first, saying I wanted to help him, he assured me that he had it covered, and that the sunshine would do me good.

He was right. I haven't been this relaxed in ages, and I actually lose myself in the book I'm reading. So much so that I don't even notice when my mother approaches.

"I heard there's some gala event for you on Friday." She's standing behind my head, casting a shadow onto my book. "Something about your book and that movie."

I grimace, then close the book, my finger marking my place. I don't look up at her. I'm not pulling a muscle in my neck for this woman. "That's right."

She sniffs. "Look at me when you speak to me."

"Your legs work. You want to see my face, nothing's stopping you."

For a brief, glorious moment, I think I've won and that she's going to simply turn around and go away. But luck is not on my side. Instead, she does what I suggested, circling my lounger and then sitting on the edge of the one just a few feet from my side.

"You didn't invite me or your father."

"Stepfather. And no. I didn't."

"Hmm. Well, I suppose it's just as well. We wouldn't be able to come anyway."

I consider asking her why she brought it up in the first place, but I know the answer: It's one more thing she can hold up as evidence of what a horrible daughter I am.

I know she's waiting for me to ask why they wouldn't be able to come. Instead, I reopen my book.

"Your father's trip got extended," she says, the word *father* making me seethe. Then again, she can call him whatever she wants so long as he doesn't have to be at the house. The fact that he's still busy overseas is perfectly fine by me.

"He has some diplomatic conference in Berlin," she continues, as if I care. "I'm flying over tonight to meet him in Nice, and I'll be staying on the Cote

D'Azur while he goes to the conference. Then we're going to take some time together in Dubai."

I gape at her as she runs all of this down, wondering why on earth she would possibly think that I care. I wait for her to continue, figuring there must be more, and when there isn't, I put on my biggest, most false smile then say, "That's a pity. I was joking before," I lie. "I actually was going to get you both tickets."

"Oh. Well. You shouldn't go to the trouble."

"It's no trouble. And it's a really big deal. I want my parents there. I know how proud you must be of me." I flash a simpering smile, then start counting. It only takes eight seconds before she turns me down flat.

"Certainly not that big a deal. I heard that they're only screening the trailer. And the gala is surely more about the movie that's premiering than your little demo real."

"Oh, no," I say sincerely. "It's a big deal. And I really want you there." The lie comes so, so easily.

"Well, Zelda, you know you can't have everything just because you want it. And you certainly can't expect other people to just bend to your will. How ridiculous to even think we would miss a visit to France and Dubai for less than five minutes of screen time and a cheap glass of champagne."

"Of course, I understand. France and Dubai are once in a lifetime opportunities." I frown, then tilt my head as if working out a particularly hard math problem. "Except for you and Daddy Dearest. You've been, what? Over a dozen times now? I can't help but wonder what there is that you haven't already seen."

Her eyes narrow. "I don't really need your sarcasm, young lady. And you would do well to remember that I'm your mother."

"Believe me," I say, "I know exactly who you are." She stands, looming over me, and I see irritation in her eyes. Not anger, not rage, but irritation. Like I'm not even worth getting worked up about. Just a little bug that's gotten in her way.

I feel Jasper's hand on my shoulder. I hadn't even heard him approach. I turn my head, drawing strength from his presence. And the fierce determination on his face.

"Problem?"

"My daughter and I were just talking."

"How nice for you," he says. "You'll have to excuse us, though. We have plans. I would say it was nice to see you, Mrs. Malloy, but we both know I'd be lying."

I stand, turning my back to my mother as I try hard to hold in my laughter.

"I love you," I whisper as we hurry back to the cottage, managing to barely get through the door before we both burst into peals of laughter. I flop onto the couch, still giggling.

He comes over and takes my hands. I tug him toward me. "Oh, no. Plans, remember?"

"Really? I thought you made that up."

"I'm taking you out."

"Really? You think that's safe?"

"I'll keep an eye out for a tail. But I doubt someone is waiting at the Getty Center to take you out."

I know I'm smiling like an idiot, but I love the Getty Center. "That sounds wonderful," I say. "And normal," I add. "Right now, I'm all about the normal."

I change into a sundress and sandals, hurrying since he's already dressed in khakis and a T-shirt. Then we take a circuitous route to the Getty Center parking.

It takes us twice as long as it should to get there, but I know he's making sure we're not being followed. Probably unnecessary, but I appreciate the care.

Once there, we ride the tram to the top. That had been one of my favorite things to do as a kid. I never went with my mother, but Tricia took me four or five times, each time tacking the visit on to a school clothes excursion because my parents seemed to think that taking me out for anything other than basic necessities was a ridiculous waste of time.

Once on the grounds of the stunning museum, we take our time. There's no way to get through this entire exhibit in one day, and so we pick and choose what we want to see. There's a visiting

Michelangelo exhibit in one of the halls, and we go there first, suffering through the line so that we can see the incredible paintings and drawings.

After that, we wander through a medieval section, something that's always fascinated me. But the truth is, my mind is wandering today. I love it here, but my head is more on Jasper than the exhibits. And when we finally decide to grab a coffee and wander through the garden, I'm giddy at the prospect.

"We should have brought snacks," I say as we follow paths through the colorful plants and lovely water features. At one point, we're holding hands and walking when Jasper leans over to kiss me. It starts out as a casual kiss but turns into something deeper. So deep, in fact, that I'm thinking it's time to head back home.

When he pulls away, he's grinning at me. I grin back, then jump when I hear someone clear their throat. I look up, only to see a woman standing a few yards away, her brow furrowed in a scowl.

"I don't think she approves," Jasper says, taking my hand and walking in the opposite direction.

"Just ignore her."

"It's because I'm so much older than you," he says.

"Just ignore her," I repeat.

"We're going to get this a lot, Zelda. We can't ignore everybody."

I stop walking and tug him to a stop, too. I hold

him there, then look into his eyes. "If you're telling me that this is really a problem, then we need to talk about it now. Because I thought we were past all that. I don't care about the years between us."

"It will be different when you're older. I'll be older, too."

"Good on you with the math. And yes. It will be different. Different isn't bad. So shut up about it or tell me this is over. Because I'm fine. But if you have a problem, then I need to know now.

He grins. "I love you," he says.

"I know. The question is what are you going to do about it?"

For a moment, he doesn't do anything, and I'm genuinely afraid that he's going to walk. That our lovely day at The Getty is going to turn into something horrible.

Then he looks over my shoulder. I frown, confused, and glance that way too. That same woman is behind us, still with the disapproving eyes.

Jasper turns his attention back to me, then he steps closer reaches around and pinches my ass.

"What the—"

But I don't get to finish the question because he pulls me close and kisses me so hard and deep I can't help but moan. His hands cup my ass and squeeze. I would laugh, but I can't with his mouth on mine and his tongue teasing me. Not to mention that I'm far too turned on for laughter.

He's putting a show on for the woman, of course, and when he pulls away, leaving me breathless, he takes my hand, and we start walking toward her. And then, right as we reach her, I see him wink.

I'm laughing as we start back to the parking lot, still reliving the moment in my mind. "You are evil," I say.

He shakes his head. "Nope. Only giving her an introduction to reality. Poor thing's probably never had a date in her life."

I giggle. "You may be right."

"Home? Or do you want to go somewhere else?"

I take his hand as we step off the tram. "I want to go home." I squeeze his fingers. "Can you guess why?"

He doesn't say anything, but he pulls me to him. "I'm sorry," he says. "It does bother me. But only because I want more time with you. I want all the time. And there's this gap. And we've already lost so much time."

"Then you'll just have to stay in incredible shape. And we'll have to make the best use of every single minute."

He grins. "I love you."

"I love you, too. But more than that, you make me happy."

"I think that's the way it's supposed to work."

"Yeah? Well, then I guess we're working just

great." We're holding hands, parting only when we reach the car. He opens the door for me, then goes to the driver's side.

As he slides in, his phone buzzes. He pulls it out, checks his texts, and mutters a soft curse.

"What's wrong?" He just shakes his head, then taps the phone to open an attached file. From my angle I can't see anything other than that it's a photograph. But I can tell from his face that it's not good.

"What happened?" I ask, at the same time he murmurs, "Oh, fuck," his voice so low that I know he doesn't even realize I'm in the car anymore. He's somewhere else. Somewhere horrible. And I don't understand what's happened.

Gently, I take the phone from him, relieved when he doesn't protest. The photo is of a woman sprawled out under a desk on cheap carpet, a bullet hole in her forehead.

I fight a wave of nausea, then close the photo and go back to the original text message. It's from someone named Liesl, with no last name in his contacts.

I went to check on her like you asked. I'm so sorry. This is what I found. — L

CHAPTER SEVENTEEN

I have zero idea what's going on. Obviously, something bad. A picture of a dead woman is rarely good. And I can tell that he's upset. What I don't know is if this is a friend, a colleague, or someone who got in the crossfire of one of his assignments.

But I'm not going to ask now. Whatever's going on, he obviously needs time to process it. So do I, for that matter.

Which is why all I do as we drive is reach my hand over and rest it gently on his thigh. He turns, gives me a soft, distracted smile, and puts his hand over mine. He leaves it there for the rest of the drive, moving it only when he needs to put it on the steering wheel.

When we finally drive through the gate and onto the property, he squeezes my fingers, then looks at me after he's killed the engine. "I'm sorry," he says.

"I don't think you have anything to be sorry about." I study his face, see the pain there, and feel completely helpless. "Is there anything I can do? You don't have to tell me, but if you want to talk about it, I'm good at listening."

I see a smile flicker on his lips and relish the feel of his hand holding mine. "I know you are."

We sit for a moment, then he draws in a breath and lets it out slowly. "She was my lead. The best lead I'd come across in ten years. She's the reason that I moved to the States. She used to work for a man named Raleigh. Once, to pay a debt, he gave her to a man they called The Maestro."

I shake my head, trying to follow this story, but I don't have any points of reference. "To use? Like sex?"

"Yes, but worse. He likes pain."

I cringe. When I ask my next question, my voice is softer. "So the Maestro is like some gang leader."

"Something like that. Nobody knows his true identity, but his codename has been going around the underworld for years. He's violent and cruel and vengeful. And he hurts women for pleasure. He hurt Melinda. Raleigh, the bookkeeper, knew that would happen, and yet he gave her to him anyway. To use. In payment of his own damn debt." His voice cracks. "That girl went through so much. And yet she helped me."

"How did she help you?"

"When I was investigating Sandra's and Bonnie's deaths, her name came up. I thought she'd been involved. I tracked her down. I cornered her. I made her talk. She told me the story. What had happened with her and Raleigh and The Maestro. She told me that Raleigh had moved to the States. And since he did bookkeeping work for The Maestro, I came here too. That's part of the reason I joined Stark Security. I keep hitting dead ends. Damien Stark's money has bought Stark Security some of the best resources in the world. Signing on and having access was my best bet for finding the deep resources I need to track the bastard down."

"Have you been able to?"

"Not yet. I had a lead, a solid one. But it didn't pan out." He pulls his hand out of mine, then clutches the steering wheel.

"Why not?" I can't believe he would just drop a lead that could help him find Bonnie and Sandra's killer.

"It's complicated. But it wasn't something I could pursue. At any rate, it didn't have anything to do with Melinda. Not really."

"Okay. So she told you about Raleigh and The Maestro, and now she's dead?"

"Yes, but I don't think that she died because she told me. That's been a while."

"What, then?"

"Recently, she got a phone call. Someone told her to call and tell me that Raleigh was dead." I nod, letting him know I understand, and wait for him to continue.

"Whoever called her told her to give me a message and a number. If I called the number, that would lead me to The Maestro."

I feel a chill and hug myself before asking, "Did you call?"

"Yes."

I wait for him to continue, but he doesn't.

"Well? What happened?"

"The lead didn't go anywhere." He sighs. "But I was concerned about Melinda. I didn't like her being back in all of this. So I asked a friend to go check on her."

"Liesl," I say. "The one from the text."

"Yes. She's an old friend. I trust her completely." He shoots me a meaningful glance, and I interpret that as meaning that she's a friend that he's occasionally slept with. I draw in a breath and tell myself that we're in a different place now. And if this woman has information to help him find Sandra and Bonnie, I have no business being jealous.

"Go on," I say.

"Liesl went to check on her. And when she got there, that's what she found."

"What's scrawled on the paper by her head?" I ask. The picture was too small on his phone for me to see, but I know that he's pinched the picture open.

"It says, 'You know what to do. If you don't, then she's only the first.'"

Now I turn my whole body to gape at him. "What does that mean?"

"I don't know exactly," he says, but he doesn't quite meet my eyes. "The only thing I'm certain of is that Melinda's not the only person who's going to die at this bastard's hands."

"But you'll stop him. You'll gather the cavalry at Stark Security, and you'll stop him."

"At this point, I don't know how."

"Is it The Maestro who's doing this?"

"I think so. I don't know who else it would be. Either The Maestro or someone whose strings he's pulling."

I drag my hands down my thighs, rubbing my sweaty palms on my floral sundress. "And what about the other part? Where he says you know what to do. What are you going to do about that?"

He turns and looks at me, and for a full two seconds, he says nothing, then he swallows and looks back out the front of the car. "What can I do? I don't know what he's talking about."

I feel ill. I don't believe him. I fear that he's been tasked to do something horrible that he doesn't want to tell me about. Something that will break a man like Jasper who I know has a deep moral code. And I know that he's already a little bit broken from the death of this woman who was helping him.

I reach out and take his hand again, relieved when he squeezes back. "You can talk to me," I say. "Whatever it is, you can tell me about it. We can work this out together. You can talk to Ryan or any of the guys at Stark Security. They have a good team there, and you're part of it. They can help you. Whatever this asshole wants from you, you don't have to handle it on your own. That's why you came here, remember?"

He strokes my hair. "I remember. Will you remember something for me?"

"Of course."

He leans forward, then gives me the sweetest kiss. When he pulls away, his smile is sad. "I love you," he says. "I love you desperately."

"Now you're scaring me." I swallow. "Jasper, if you're going to disappear on me, don't."

"I'm not going to disappear on you."

"Because I can't stand somebody else leaving. You know that."

He squeezes my hand. "I'm not going anywhere. I'm staying right here. I've made my decision."

I want to ask him what that means exactly, but

there's a car pulling up behind us in the driveway. There aren't that many people who can get into the driveway without authorization, so I watch it, surprised when I see that it's Ryan.

Leah's in the passenger side, though, and since she has the gate code, that explains how they're here. As soon as Ryan parks the car, they both get out.

I exchange glances with Jasper, and he looks as confused as I feel. We start to get out of the car, but before we do, Jasper grasps my hand and squeezes it tight. "Do you have any idea how grateful I am to have you in my life?"

"Probably as grateful as I am to have you." I wish we were alone. I can tell that he's been shaken by Melinda's death, and all I want to do is get him inside and hold him close. Apparently, though, there's work to be done first.

Ryan is uncharacteristically quiet, and Leah doesn't quite look at me as we enter the house. I offer them both something to drink, but they turn it down, choosing instead to sit at the dining room table. Jasper and I follow suit.

I'm nervous, and I have no idea why. "What's going on?" I finally ask. "You both are acting very strange." A wave of fear crashes over me. "Wait. Did someone die?" It's the only thing I can think of that would feel this somber, and suddenly I want to throw up.

"Please," I say. "Just tell us fast."

Across the table, Leah meets Ryan's eyes.

Ryan's shoulders rise, then fall, and he draws a breath before speaking. "Jasper," he finally says, his voice hard and cold. "I know."

CHAPTER EIGHTEEN

"**Y**ou know," I repeat, gaping at Ryan. "What is it that you think you know?"

I look between Ryan and Jasper, and suddenly it hits me. *Of course.* Jasper's been using Stark Security resources to investigate The Maestro. Ryan's pissed. And maybe Ryan even knows about Melinda's death.

He's probably going to lecture Jasper on the risks of blow back to the agency for the kinds of investigations that Jasper's running on his own.

I reach out and grasp Jasper's hand under the table, offering my silent support. Except he won't take it. Instead, he pulls his hand away.

I glance over, and that's when I see the expression on his face. That's when I realize I'm wrong. I don't know what's going on, but this is about a hell of a lot more than utilizing Stark Security resources without authorization.

"Tell me," I say to Jasper. "What's going on?"

"You're not going to like this," Ryan says to me. "Leah. Play it."

Leah meets my eyes, and I see that hers are full of apology. Then she puts her phone on the table. "This recording came to us today. We've only had time to do a cursory forensic examination, but it looks legit." She glances at Ryan, who nods. "We don't know who the other voice is," she adds, "but you'll both recognize one speaker."

She looks at me again, then drops her gaze.

Cold terror runs through me. I have no idea what's going on, but I know it's going to be bad. Beside me, Jasper's palms are flat on the table. He looks perfectly calm, and in that moment, I realize what a good agent he must be. I think about all the things he must have seen in the course of his career. And about how many lies he must have told in order to keep himself alive.

"Just start it already," I snap.

She does, and I listen to the horrible words being spewed out from the tiny speaker.

This is Jasper Kent. I got a message to call this number.

I search his face for a reaction. There isn't one. Not recognition, not remorse, not anything. He is stone.

And that scares me to death.

Kill her. Kill her, or others will die, too.

I hug myself, trying to place the low raspy

voice. It sounds familiar, and yet unfamiliar at the same time. Like something out of a nightmare.

Kill her? That's Jasper's voice. *Melinda?*

Melinda's the girl in the text he just got. Is he the one who killed her? Was his shock from being caught and from seeing her dead?

Surely not. He's been in the States, and Melinda's in London.

Kill Zelda Clayton.

Bile rises in my throat, and a wave of panic almost knocks me out of my chair.

Kill her, and I'll tell you where to find The Maestro.

I can't help it. Everything in my stomach rises up my throat. I lurch out of the chair, trying to make it to the kitchen sink, because I know I can't make it to the bathroom.

I vomit, barely getting there in time, and then I sink to the ground, grabbing a towel off the counter as I do and clutching it to my mouth.

I don't know how he got there so fast, but Jasper is right by my side, his hands on my knees. "Are you okay? Zelda, I'm so sorry. Are you okay?" He tries to pull me close, and I reach out and slap him so hard across the cheek my palm goes numb.

"Get out of here." My voice is raw from the acid from my stomach and from my anger. "Just get the hell out of my house."

"Zelda, baby, please. I wouldn't. I didn't. I could never hurt you."

I close my eyes, trying to wish him away. But beneath the black curtain of my vision, I remember his hand at my throat during sex. I remember standing at the edge of a cliff off Mulholland Drive. I can imagine how tempted he must have been. One push and he'd have his answers, none of which could bring back the dead.

"Get away from me," I say. My voice is mine again, but it's hard and cold, and I don't recognize it. I'm broken. This man has broken me.

I hear the scrape of the chair as Ryan pushes back from the table. He stands and walks over to me. He kneels beside me, and his voice is calm when he says, "Zelda, I'm so very sorry. You probably hate me now, but you had to know."

"You son of a bitch," Jasper says.

Ryan and I both ignore him. I look at Ryan and nod. "Thank you," I say, my voice tremulous. "Please go."

"Leah is going to stay here with you." I shake my head. I want to be alone.

"I'm not taking no for an answer," he says. "And Leah and I are both stronger than you. She's staying."

"Fine. Whatever." I'm going to go close my eyes and go to sleep for a year, so what does it matter anyway?

With a sigh, I stand up. I draw a breath. Then I flinch when Jasper reaches for me, his eyes filled with horror and remorse. I turn away, afraid I'll throw up again if I look at him.

I glance at Leah, who holds out her hand, offering me comfort. I turn away and stalk to my bedroom. I consider climbing out the window just to get away, but I don't have the energy.

I feel dead inside. Lost. I love him, and he did this to me. And I still love him, and it hurts. Now all I want to do is hate him, and I can't help but wonder how long it's going to take for that to happen.

I curl up on top of the covers and roll the comforter over on top of me. My knees are at my chest, and I'm in a little cocoon, crying into my pillow.

I felt like a new person when Jasper had come into my life. I felt like the me I had pretended to be out in the world, bubbly and alive, not dark and twisty. Now I'm dark again, and I'm twisted up inside.

Mostly, I'm gone, shattered into a million pieces.

But maybe that's better. I'd been living in the real world before. My time with Jasper was a fantasy. I know that now. I know the truth. Everybody leaves. Everybody disappoints. And I'm better off just staying alone.

CHAPTER NINETEEN

J asper paced in his hotel room. A new one, empty of clothes or toiletries or personal belongings. All of his things were still at Zelda's cottage.

Zelda.

God, what had he done?

He'd fucked up.

He'd fucked up royally, and he knew it. He knew he deserved to lose her. That he'd betrayed her. Not physically, but he'd betrayed her trust. And now she was gone.

He supposed he was lucky he still had a job. Ryan had insisted they go to the Stark Security offices, and Jasper hadn't been in any position to say no. So he'd followed his boss back to the agency, where Ryan had reamed him in front of everybody who'd been in the office at the time.

Told them the whole story. Rolled out his

shame.

And then Ryan had announced that he was on probation. Not because he'd hurt Zelda—Ryan knew damn well that Jasper hadn't hurt her and never would.

No, the probation was because he hadn't gone to Ryan or anyone at the agency about the ultimatum.

Now he was on paperwork duty. But at least he was still employed. That was good. If he didn't have a job, he didn't know what he would do. He didn't need the money, but he did need the distraction. Because he'd lost Zelda, and without work, his days would be filled with nothing more than pain and loss.

God, he'd fucked up bad.

"It will get better," Trevor said. The other agent was sitting on the end of the hotel bed, looking at Jasper like he might explode.

"You can go. I'm not a time bomb."

"No. I'll stay. You might want to talk."

Jasper considered telling the agent to get the hell out of the hotel room. That he didn't want to talk, and if he did, it wouldn't be to Trevor.

He hated that Trevor and Simon and Quince in particular knew his shame. Knew that for even a moment, he had actually considered killing Zelda. He hadn't said so out loud, but the fact that he hadn't revealed the demand to anyone at Stark Security spoke volumes.

The rest of the agents didn't matter as much. Not yet. He hadn't had a chance to meet them personally, other than Leah, and at least she was a shoulder for Zelda to cry on. Zelda deserved that.

But he'd worked side by side with Quince in London. And Trevor and Simon had been at the party. They'd laughed together, played stupid games together, got drunk together. And now, for them to see his flaws...

He shuddered.

"I should have told her," he said. "If I'd only told Zelda, none of this would have happened. She would've understood. I'm certain of it."

"Were you certain of it back then?"

"I don't know. Maybe not. I should've been. It was so new. It's still so new. But what I feel for her. It's so real. But I thought ... I don't know what I thought. Maybe I was afraid of burdening her with it."

"Or maybe you were considering it. Killing her, I mean." Trevor looked him in the eye and said nothing else. Just waited.

He closed his eyes, his throat thick. "I did. I really did. For so long I've been trying to find the path to get vengeance for Sandra and Bonnie. And then there it was, in the palm of my hand. Exactly what I was looking for. Only in order to get it, I had to dive into hell. I'd lost the family I loved."

He opened his eyes and looked straight at

Trevor's. "And to make that right, I was going to have to kill the woman I'd fallen in love with."

"I get it," Trevor said. "Of course, you considered it. But considering isn't the same as doing."

"But I should've told her. I should have admitted I was tempted. And I should've trusted her enough to understand that I would never actually go through with it."

God help him, he *had* been tempted. But he would never have done it. Zelda had stolen his heart the moment he saw her in that gold dress. She hadn't pushed Sandra and Bonnie out of his heart; she'd just filled a new and empty space. He would always love them, but he couldn't be with them.

Zelda was alive and vibrant and beautiful. She fit him, so perfectly. And he'd screwed it all up, simply because he had to keep his goddamn mouth shut.

"Seriously, man. You need to forgive yourself."

He scoffed, then shook his head. "I really don't think you get it."

"Yeah? You think I don't understand what it's like to have something you want to tell someone? To be too scared to do it because you don't know how they're going to react, and if they react badly, you'll lose everything with them? That suddenly they'll be out of your life completely? You think I don't understand that?"

Jasper took a step back, surprised by the force of his friend's words. He remembered the party. The way Trevor looked at Ollie. The way he brought him fresh drinks, and they'd laughed together. And Ollie, so incredibly smart, was also so incredibly clueless.

"Sorry," he said. "I guess you do get it."

Trevor raised his brows. "Yeah, well, one day maybe I'll say something."

"Don't worry, I won't say anything before you do."

"I know. Hell, you don't even have the balls to tell Zelda."

"Fuck you."

Trevor grinned, and then they both laughed.

"Thanks," Jasper said when the laughter died down. "I didn't want an escort, but I'm glad you came."

Trevor nodded. "Truly not a problem. But what are you going to do now?"

"I'm going to do whatever I have to do to keep Zelda safe. Nothing has changed there. Whoever wanted Melinda dead also wants Zelda dead."

"But who?" Trevor asked. "Run me through it. Who are your suspects?"

"I have a very long list of hardly anyone," Jasper said. "It all boils down to this Maestro. He ties into this for sure, but I don't know why he would want Zelda dead."

"Probably to get at you. He's probably been watching you. Realizes how you feel about her. Wants to make sure that you're going to perform."

"Possible. That's very possible." He paced the hotel room, his mind whirring.

"But?"

He paused in his pacing long enough to lift a shoulder. "But it doesn't quite feel right. I can't put my finger on it. I'm not dismissing it, I just feel like we're missing something."

"You may not figure it out tonight. You've been through the wringer, my friend. We should get some sleep and jump in tomorrow."

"You're right."

"You need anything? Do you want me to run back to Zelda's and get your stuff?"

"No. Thank you, though. I've got a hotel robe here. I'll put my clothes out to launder overnight. I don't want her to have to think about me. Not now. Not while it still hurts."

Trevor stood. "It's going to work out. You two are good together. I'm rooting for you."

"You are far too chipper, my friend," Jasper said, managing a grin.

"All right, I'm out of here. Call me if you need anything."

"I don't have your number handy."

"Right. I'll text it to you."

Trevor tapped on his phone, and then Jasper's pinged. He glanced down and saw that he'd received a new text.

"Now I'm really out of here," Trevor said, stepping out of the room and letting the door close behind him.

Alone, Jasper started to strip, planning to get into the robe and call housekeeping to come deal with his clothes. But before he did, he opened the text out of habit. When he did that, he saw the text from Liesl. He winced, wishing he hadn't opened the goddamn app.

He tossed his phone on the bed, cursing it. Then he cursed himself, crossed to the bed, and picked it back up. He opened the image, making it bigger and bigger, looking at Melinda's face, searching for clues. He didn't know what he was looking for, but he went over every pixel of that damn photograph.

And then he saw it.

It was near where the paper lay. The threat that said Melinda would just be the first if Jasper didn't kill Zelda.

Wasn't happening, which meant Jasper needed to find another way. A way to track down the Maestro. A way to kill the bastard.

And maybe—just maybe—he'd found a path.

He zoomed in on the tiny flash of color, once again grateful that the picture was high definition. It was blurry and familiar, but he wasn't quite sure what he was looking at.

Then he realized it was a cigar band, a cigar band that featured a colorful background and a vibrant red parrot.

CHAPTER TWENTY

I'm trying to sleep, but not even managing to doze, when I hear the sharp tap at my door. "Go away," I say. The tap turns into a pounding knock. I roll over in my cocoon, wrapping the comforter around my ears. "Go. Away."

"I'm not going anywhere." Leah's voice is firm.

"Just leave me alone. I want to sleep."

"We need to talk."

I groan and sit up. "What part of no don't you understand?"

"Never mind. I'm coming in."

I hear the doorknob rattle, followed by her soft curse when she realizes that I locked it. I allow myself a smug smile and do another turn in my cocoon of comforters, covering my ears for when she's going to inevitably start yelling at me again.

But the yelling doesn't come.

I try to fall back asleep, but I can't because I keep expecting her to knock at the door.

I'm irritated. Irritated at Leah for not leaving me alone, at Ryan for starting all of this, and at Jasper for making me love him.

Damn it, damn it, damn it.

The only one not filling my mind is this damn Maestro, and he's the one I should be angry at. But how can I be angry at a chimera? Some evil criminal overlord who's completely fucked up my life.

I groan and squeeze my eyes shut, hoping that a witch will put a spell on me and I can pull a Sleeping Beauty. Right now, that's all I want. To sleep. To forget.

I think I might actually be drifting off when I hear the scrape of metal at my door. I sit up, trying to figure out what I'm hearing. By the time I realize that she's picking the lock, it's already open.

Leah stands there in the doorway, her arms crossed as she stares me down. "That's a really shitty lock you have."

"No one asked you to come in. And what the hell are you doing in here, anyway? My door was locked. Ergo, no invitation."

"I'll go away. But we're going to talk first."

I make a low growling noise but loosen my cocoon so I can scoot back, propping myself against the headboard. I stay snuggled in my blankets, though. I want the warmth. I want the protection.

"Fine," I say. "Talk. Dance. Do whatever you want. Anything. Just get it over with so I can sleep."

"Why are you so pissed?"

"Because you're not letting me sleep."

"No. I mean at him. Why are you so pissed at Jasper?"

I gape at her. "You're kidding, right? What conversation were you just listening to? The man was supposed to kill me."

"And yet here you are, living and breathing and being annoying."

"What the hell is your problem?" The words slam out of me, my temper flaring. "He didn't tell me anything that was going on, and now you're mad at me because I'm mad at him? You wouldn't be?"

"Maybe. A little. But you're acting like he *did* kill you. He didn't, and we both know he wouldn't. He would never hurt you. Damn it, Zelda, he worships you. Don't you see that? You've become his whole world. He loves you. And, damn it, you need him. He's brought you into the sun."

I feel my eyes fill with hot, annoying, inconvenient tears. "He was supposed to kill me," I say. "And he thought about it. I know he did. His hands at my throat. Standing near the edge on Mulholland. I didn't realize it then, but I know what he was thinking. That it would be so easy. So easy to just push me over and have his answers."

Slowly, she nods. Then she takes a step toward

me and sits on the edge of the bed, her hand extended. After a moment, I put my hand in hers.

"I'm sorry," she says. "That must feel terrible. Knowing that he thought about it. Knowing that for a moment, he looked at the possibility of having the answer to a question that's haunted him for ten years. For one moment, he held the key to finding out who killed Sandra and Bonnie. He had it. But then he tossed it away, and do you know why?"

I shake my head, because even though I do know the answer, I can't bring myself to say it, or to even think it. Not really.

I taste saltwater, and realize tears are streaming down my face.

"He thought about it, yes. But he *chose* you."

"Maybe he did, but he still fucked up. He should have told me."

"Maybe. Maybe not. He was trained as a spy. Do you know what that means?"

I don't answer.

She grimaces. "Okay. How about this—do you believe he loves you?"

"I don't know."

She barks out a laugh. "That is such bullshit."

"What is your problem?" I snap.

"Honestly? You. You are my problem. Right now, you are the only problem I've got. And you're a big one."

"Why are you picking on me? This is the worst

day of my life. The man I love thought about killing me."

"And he didn't because he loves you." She drags her fingers through her hair. "This is the problem. You say that people leave you, but do they really? Do you even try to meet them halfway? Did you ever try with Camille?"

"What? Why are we talking about Camille? I can barely have a conversation with her now."

"Because you two never connected after she moved away. And yes, that's partly her fault, but she tried. She told me she reached out a couple of times, and you never seemed interested. You were just angry that she was gone. And by the time you got over it, she'd moved on. Maybe she shouldn't have, maybe she should have tried harder after you had a chance to deal, but it wasn't entirely her fault."

My eyes are wide, and I'm feeling the force of her words like a slap. "I... I..."

I shake my head, realizing I can't say anything because I'm crying. "I'm sorry."

Her shoulders droop. "It's not really about Camille. You're both doing fine. That's not the point. The point is Jasper. If you love him, you have to meet him halfway. Especially if you believe he loves you too. So that's the question," she said. "Are you giving up? Or are you going to fight for him?"

CHAPTER TWENTY-ONE

It had taken all of Jasper's willpower to wait until morning, and he'd had to talk himself out of going to the bastard's house at least five times during the night. Better to go to the office, anyway. He wanted witnesses.

He wanted everyone at Stark Security to know what that little worm Owen had done. And he wanted witnesses when he forced the prick to explain why he'd taken that poor woman's life.

He crossed The Domino's pavilion, watching the Santa Monica business park come to life. Most people were clustered around the coffee cart, enjoying the morning before they started their workday.

But Jasper had a mission. And today, he really didn't need caffeine.

He headed to Stark Security, the anchor tenant for the complex, then held back as two agents he didn't recognize entered. When he saw that no one else was approaching the door, he hurried over, drew a breath, then yanked open the door and crossed the threshold.

He paused, feeling all eyes on him. He was on official probation as of this morning per the email Ryan had distributed before midnight. No field-work. Grunt-style computer research and data entry for the next three months.

That was fine by Jasper.

Hell, in an hour he might not even have that as a job. But being fired was a small price to pay to avenge Melinda's life.

He ignored the whispers as he crossed to Owen's workspace. The office was still mostly empty. It was only eight, and most agents didn't arrive until nine or later, the job tending to call for late nights, after all.

Owen pushed a desk, however, and he was right where he was supposed to be, his eyes full of curiosity as Jasper came closer and closer, until finally they were barely a foot apart. That's when Jasper lashed out with one hell of a left hook and got the traitorous prick right in the jaw.

Owen stumbled back, his mouth bleeding. He fell against his rolling chair and went down.

Jasper didn't think. Hell, he wasn't even in his body. All he knew—all that existed—was the fight. He was on top of Owen, pounding the lousy prick's face, landing hard blows to his chest, doing whatever he could to cause damage before the other agents in the room dragged him off.

It didn't take long.

Less than thirty seconds later, two of the security staff had ripped him off of Owen and cuffed his hands behind his back. Someone shouted that Ryan was in the parking garage, and all the while, Jasper stood there with a smile on his face, watching Owen bleeding and in pain on the floor.

"What the hell?" Leah shouted, grabbing Jasper's arm and shaking him. His balance was off from the cuffs, and he stumbled against Owen's desk, then snapped his attention to Leah.

"He killed her. That noxious little worm killed Melinda."

"Everyone, back to work." Ryan's voice rang through the room, and the lingering staff scattered. "Leah, you stay. Is he okay?" Ryan asked with a nod to Owen, who was on the floor with Quincy, who'd grabbed a First aid kit.

"He'll be fine. Sore. But fine." Quincy shot Jasper a curious look but didn't say anything. Just continued to treat Owen, who looked far too healthy for Jasper's taste.

"Seriously, Jasper," Leah snapped. "What the fuck?" She glanced up at Ryan. "Sorry. I'll stay quiet."

"No. That was my exact question."

"He killed Melinda Barrett. A source. The first and only solid lead I've had in my investigation as to who killed my wife and daughter." He forced his voice to stay level. Professional. Though why he was bothering, he wasn't sure. He'd already blown professional all to hell.

"If that's true, I'd probably have done the same thing," Ryan said. "So what's your proof?"

He jangled his cuffs. "Easier to tell if I can also show."

Ryan signaled to Leah, who uncuffed him. He rolled his shoulders, then glared at Owen.

"Don't even think about it," Ryan said. "You two, in the conference room. Opposite sides of the table. You even think about getting into it, and I will have you in a detention cell so fast it will make your head spin. Quincy, you too."

"We'll be joining the conference, too."

Ollie's familiar voice came from near the door, and Jasper's heart skipped a beat as he looked up to see Zelda standing there with Ollie beside her, both in jogging shorts.

"I don't think that's a good idea," Ryan began, but Zelda cut him off. "You're the one who assigned him to protect me, and yesterday I learned that he'd been tasked to kill me. So yeah, I think it is necessary. Unless you want to give me a chance to talk to him now."

Jasper held his breath, hoping Ryan agreed. He needed to talk to her. Needed to figure out a way to get them back on track. But at the same time, if she was making a clean break from him, he'd just as soon postpone the pain.

"Fine," Ryan said. "You can come in, but you're only observing. But not Ollie."

"Yes, Ollie," she retorted. "Consider him my counsel."

Ryan looked like he wanted to argue, but instead he turned to Jasper. "Objections?"

"No. Whatever she wants," he said, pleasantly surprised when she met his eyes and didn't turn away until Ryan urged them into the room. Jasper and Owen were seated at opposite ends of the oval table, with Zelda and Ollie on one side, and Ryan on the other.

"I don't even know where to start," Ryan said, shooting Jasper an exasperated look.

"Start with this," Jasper said. "Look especially by the table leg. Have him explain that."

He passed Ryan his phone, open to the picture of Melinda.

Ryan studied it, then passed it to Owen, who sent it around to Zelda, who winced at the photo, and then gave the phone to Ollie.

"I'm sorry about the girl," Owen said." But what does that have to do with me?"

"That message on the paper is for me. Trying to coerce me into killing Zelda. Warning me that if I didn't, others would die."

He was looking at Owen, but he could still see Zelda hugging herself, and he hated that his words were causing her pain.

As for Owen, his only reaction was confusion.

"Coerce?" Ryan repeated. "We received an anonymous tip last night. From what I understand, you don't need coercion to kill. Just a healthy paycheck and a lust for the freelance lifestyle."

"Seriously?" His temper spiked, his blood positively boiling. "You want to go there? Fine, let's go there." He paused long enough to glance at Zelda. This was the part he hadn't told her yet, but there was no avoiding it now. "Yeah, I left MI6 to go freelance. And yeah, I've been contracted for some hits. But I choose my clients, and I investigate the target. I make sure the reasons are sound, and that the justice system has fucked them over."

"You're saying you have a conscience."

"Don't you dare lay into me about that," he snapped. "I'm not in that business anymore, and if we're going to have that talk, then I need to not be the only one on the firing line. You know damn well what your other agents have done before they signed up. Or do we need to ask Quincy and Simon to step into the room?"

He crossed his arms, forcing himself not to look to Zelda. He'd told her none of this, and he was desperately afraid that he'd just dug down another six feet in his own damn grave.

"You've made your point, and you're right. We're not interested in your freelance career before joining us. But we are interested in the fact that someone offered you payment to kill Zelda."

"Payment?"

"Information about your family's killer," Ryan said, his voice so level that it took all of Jasper's strength just to keep from punching him.

"I didn't ask for that, and I didn't take the assignment." He forced himself not to look at Zelda, afraid that if he did, the guilt he felt would show on his face.

He hadn't lied to Ryan—he hadn't hurt her— but he had thought about it. To his eternal shame, he'd actually considered it. If it had been anyone other than Zelda, he might even have gone through with it.

"Whoever was baiting me promised me information about Sandra's and Bonnie's deaths in exchange for killing Zelda." He lifted a chin. "That wasn't a price I was prepared to pay."

"Even though that might be your last chance?" Ryan asked.

Jasper sat up straight, his eyes locked on Ryan's. "Even so. I dropped the rope, sir. I made a choice, and I dropped the rope."

"What does that even mean?" Owen blurted.

"It means he loves me," Zelda said, and when he looked toward her, she mouthed, *I love you, too,* and her soft smile filled his soul.

Really? He asked silently, then almost floated out of his chair when she nodded.

He drew a breath, forcing himself to focus on the situation with Owen. "That paper—that message to me—isn't relevant right now. What you need to focus on is the cigar band."

"Cigar band?" Owen snorted a laugh. "That's your big bombshell? That's one of the most popular brands in the world. And to be honest, I haven't even smoked one yet. I told you they were a gift. Go open the box if you want to."

A gift.

"A gift from who?"

"My mentor at the CIA. They're his brand. He wanted me to follow in his footsteps."

"Oh, bloody hell," Jasper said. "Who was your mentor?"

Owen's brows rose. "Seriously? You're going from thinking I'm the spawn of Satan to pursuing my mentor? The guy's a legend. And he's not even in the CIA anymore. He's got his own business."

"A name," Jasper said.

"He's CIA. You know I can't reveal—"

"A name."

Owen looked to Ryan. "Are you hearing this crap?"

"Just give him the name."

"Fine. Whatever. Carter Malloy. He's a hell of a guy."

CHAPTER TWENTY-TWO

"Carter Malloy," Ollie repeated. "Carter Malloy was your mentor?"

"Yeah," Owen said. "What's the big deal?"

"Not a thing," Ollie said, in what Jasper considered a completely unbelievable tone. "I've met the man. Back when I was working for the FBI. Joint task force."

"So you know. He's had my back since I was a trainee. Helped me get in as an analyst, climb through the ranks."

"Recommended you for this job, too," Ryan said. "Almost looks like he wanted someone inside with eyes on this operation."

"No, that's not—"

"And he smokes San Cristobal Ovations," Jasper pointed out. "Lots of little things piling up. Not looking good for your buddy."

"This is bullshit," Owen said. "You have literally zero evidence."

"We know that someone wants me dead," Zelda said. "And we know that someone set up Jasper, trying to entice him to kill me. I know I'm not the most well loved person on the planet, but the odds that two people proactively want me dead seems slim. So I'm going out on a limb and saying it's the same person."

"Makes sense to me," Ollie said. "And, gee, I wonder who might stand to benefit if you die."

"Carter's my stepfather," she told Owen. "Just in case you need to catch up. And if I die, he and my mom get the land and house. Which, to be clear, is worth a fuck ton of money."

Jasper fought a smile. The woman he loved had a serious bite.

"To be fair," Ollie put in, "it's Mrs. Malloy who would inherit. But I have a feeling that's the kind of challenge that Carter Malloy can overcome in his sleep."

Owen looked at each of them in turn, finally stopping at Jasper. "You all really believe this. You think he's dirty."

"I do," Jasper said. "I think he killed Melanie. I think he tried to bait me into killing Zelda."

Owen dragged his fingers through his hair, making it stand on end. "Okay, okay. I'm listening. But this can't be right. There has to be an explanation."

"Hold up, everybody," Ollie said as he lifted his phone and shook it. "I just got something here."

Everyone at the table turned to look at him. "What is it?" Zelda asked.

"So here's the thing," Ollie said. "You know how Matthew Holt told you two about the art files for the little target icon that goes above all the chapters in the book?"

Jasper looked at Ryan, who nodded.

"Well, he gave me a call and asked me to do some follow-up. We sent a forensics team into Holt's offices, and we were able to track down an unauthorized download of that folder by a data processing team member."

"Well, that's excellent," Zelda said. "Isn't it?" She looked to Jasper, who nodded.

"I think it might be," Ollie said. "Let me walk you through it. We pinpointed the date of the download, which corresponded to twenty-four hours before the threat appeared in Zelda's mail. We also knew the location from which he downloaded it, and after watching him, we realized that he's a creature of habit. He takes the same route to and from work every day."

Jasper looked at Zelda and shrugged. He knew Ollie had a point; he just wished he would get to it.

"We had a team of agents canvas the area. Turns out he lives close and walked. This was good for us. It took some time, but we were able to check video footage at most of the locations along his regular route. ATMs, security cameras, traffic cameras, the like."

"And you found something," Zelda guessed.

"They just emailed it to me. Is there a way to project it up so everyone can see?"

"Send it to me," Ryan said, and a few minutes later they were looking at a wall screen onto which the video was projected. At first, it was just the image of a street corner somewhere in Los Angeles. Then, a man came into view.

He was tall and thin and wore his hair pulled back in a ponytail. He stood on a street corner, shifting his weight back and forth from foot to foot. It looked like someone who was either very, very nervous, or desperately needed a restroom.

A few minutes later, another man joined him, and Ponytail passed an envelope to the second man. From the angle, it was impossible to see the second man's face, and Jasper was just about to ask if there was video with an angle across the street, when the man turned.

It was Carter Malloy.

"I don't get it," Owen said. "I don't get what you're trying to say." He glared at Ollie, as if Ollie was messing up everything. Jasper guessed that from Owen's perspective, he probably was.

"It's simple," Ollie said. "Someone stole a particular file with a graphic on it from Hardline Entertainment. That graphic somehow ended up on a death threat sent to Zelda. We know that Peter

Danvoy—Mr. Ponytail in the video—accessed that folder during a time when he was not officially logged into the computer and on a station that didn't normally belong to him. We also know that on that same day, he entered into a transaction with Carter Malloy, someone we suspect might harbor ill will toward Zelda. Considering the two met, the probability is high that Carter acquired the graphics file and sent the threat to Zelda."

He cleared his throat. "That's it," he added, and everyone around the table nodded, with the exception of Owen, who still looked shell-shocked.

"There's more," Zelda said. "I just remembered it, but it supports the conclusion that Carter's involved. The other day, my mother mentioned that she was annoyed I hadn't offered to get her tickets for the gala. I didn't think anything about it at the time. My mother is constantly annoyed with me, and I mostly just tune her out. But I just realized something," she continued.

"How did she know about the gala?" Jasper said.

"Exactly." Zelda looked around the table. "The gala that's being thrown in honor of *Intercontinental* is meant to be a surprise. No one who has tickets to the real premier knows that they're going to get to see the trailer. It's an odd publicity stunt in that there is no publicity, but that's the way Holt's company wants to handle it."

"But somehow your mother knew," Jasper said.

"Probably because she heard it from your stepfather. And I'm guessing he knows because he's the one who's up to something."

Everyone at the table except Owen nodded, either absorbing the information or agreeing. And they all turned to look at the odd man out.

"Anything to say?" Jasper asked.

Slowly, Owen shook his head. "I don't want to believe it. This man has been good to me my entire life. He noticed me when I was a trainee. He got me into the freaking CIA. But everything I've seen today...."

"We know," Zelda said gently.

"I wish I could deny all of it," Owen said. "But I'm trying to be objective, and what you've shown me suggests that Carter Malloy really is dirty." He drew in a breath, looking positively miserable. "I'm sorry I doubted you."

"Don't worry about it," Zelda said. "We all have loyalty to the people we love."

Owen managed a small smile. "I appreciate that," he said. "And I think I need to tell you something else too," he said, turning to Jasper. "Honestly, I should have said something ages ago. But now, with all this stuff about Carter, well, I guess I really do need to tell you now."

"What is it?" Jasper asked.

"I knew Sandra," Owen said. "I met her about eleven years ago. I was living in London at the time, and we were both taking a class about modern art at the Tate. We hit it off, became friendly. I thought she was incredible."

Jasper felt himself go cold, and he wished that Zelda were sitting beside him instead of across the table. He felt the comfort of her gaze, but he wanted her hand in his. He wasn't sure where this conversation was going, but he had a feeling that he wasn't going to like when it got there. "Go on." he said after Owen paused.

"I, um, well, to be honest, I fell in love with her. I imagine that you can understand why."

He could barely get the words out, but he had to know. "And Sandra? How did she feel about you?"

"I, I thought she felt the same. But when I talked to her, she made it clear that she didn't. She loved you. She loved your family. And she told me that as much as she enjoyed being friends with me, it made her uncomfortable to know that I felt that way. She thought it was best if we never saw each other again."

"When was that?"

"About two months before she died. I'm so sorry. I went to the funeral. I stood back from the group, but I wanted to pay my respects. She was a wonderful woman, and she loved you very much."

"Thank you for telling me," Jasper said, though he wasn't sure that he was thankful at all. He could have gone the rest of his life without knowing that this man had intimate feelings toward his wife. And he certainly hadn't needed any proof that Sandra had been faithful. That much he'd always known in his heart.

Owen cleared his throat. "I, um, didn't decide to tell you this because we're having a warm and fuzzy moment. I'm telling you because Carter Malloy knows."

"What are you talking about?" Zelda asked.

"He mentioned once that he had a photo of me standing by Sandra's car talking to her. He said it was obvious how I felt from the expression on my face. And he said that he expected me to continue being his good protegé as I moved up through the ranks at the CIA."

He cleared his throat. "It's one of the reasons I decided to leave the Company after he did. Once he was on the outside, I was afraid that he'd expect me to share secrets. Things I wasn't supposed to take outside the office. I wasn't comfortable doing that, and so I quit. Again, it's all speculation, but now I suppose there's no doubt that he had that intention. And that says a lot about the character of a man."

"It does," Jasper said. "Thank you for letting us know."

"Yes," Ryan said. "Thank you. On a more formal note, you've both redeemed yourself in this meeting. If you two will agree to put this behind you, I don't think we need to impose any sort of formal penalties on either of you for that scene in the office. Jasper, you're still on probation for the failure to disclose."

"Yes, sir. That's a price I'm willing to pay."

Across the table, Jasper saw Zelda smile. And he counted the minutes until he could have her in his arms.

Unfortunately, as Ryan continued to talk, he realized that moment wasn't coming anytime soon. "We need a plan for figuring out how to take this man down. I want a live capture. I want him to stand trial for what he's done. And ultimately, I want a full confession. So the question is, what's our game plan?"

Ryan leaned back in the chair, surveying everyone at the table and waiting for them to come up with a response. Unfortunately, Jasper didn't have anything.

"No one?" Ryan looked at all of them. "Should we open it to the team? Get various ideas from the other agents out in the office?"

Jasper was about to say that that was a good idea, when he had a sudden brainstorm. "Maybe not just yet. I want to run this by everyone and see if it's crazy, but I have an idea. Or, to be more accurate, I have an idea of how we can come up with an idea."

They all looked at him like he'd lost it, which made sense as he certainly sounded that way. "How sure are we that he's our guy?" He looked around the table, looking hard at each of them.

"Ninety percent? Eighty? One hundred? Personally, I'm going to go with ninety-five. How about you all?"

He paused, waiting for the responses, and finally everyone agreed with him. At least in their minds, Malloy was guilty. In fact, the only one who didn't say ninety-five percent was Zelda. Her answer was ninety-nine. "I'll leave a one percent margin," she said. "But he doesn't deserve more than that."

"All right then. What's our plan?"

She frowned. "What are you talking about?"

"That's my plan," he said. "To learn what you'd do if this was a Martin King book."

She sat back, her eyes wide. "You're seriously asking me that? You're asking me what I would do in an over-the-top thriller?"

"Yep."

He thought she was going to argue. He thought she was going to tell him he was nuts. Instead, she smiled. A slow smile that lit up her entire face. "Okay," she said. "Let me think. Something bold. Something unexpected. I'm just not sure what it is yet."

"Well, the first problem to tackle is getting him here. He's currently overseas. Remember?"

"Damn," she said. "And considering what he's been up to, he's probably intending to stay there." She drummed her fingers on the table, clearly thinking.

"Which means it's not a question of how you would capture Malloy in your book," Ollie said, "It's how you would lure him back to the States."

Zelda nodded slowly. "Some sort of inter-agency operation. Big and colorful. Something that plays out with lots of action, especially if it's going to be adapted into a movie. But for this, flashy doesn't feel right. Something quick and dirty. Clever. But I don't know—*oh!*"

She looked at each of them in turn, a wide smile on her beautiful face. "I think I've got the perfect solution."

CHAPTER TWENTY-THREE

"This is going to work, right?" Zelda asked as Jasper poured some wine for her and Ollie. They'd come back to the cottage after the meeting wherein Zelda had pitched the barebones outline of her crazy idea.

Brilliant, yes. But crazy.

And just crazy enough to work.

He bent over and ran his tongue over the curve of her ear before whispering, "It will work, and you're a genius. And as soon as we can get rid of Ollie, I'm ripping off all your clothes."

"I heard that," Ollie said.

"You were supposed to. That was my subtle way of kicking you out."

Ollie laughed. "Fair enough, and I'll get out of your hair soon. I wouldn't dream of getting in the way of good sex. But something came up earlier. It can wait, but I wanted to mention it without the others around."

"Shoot."

"Just that it's good you're going legit. Your freelance work was getting more notice than you might have been aware."

Jasper frowned. "How so?"

"Remember when I said you looked familiar? I finally figured out why. I've seen photos that have been shared between the FBI and the SOC. Nobody's looking to arrest you. But they are looking. Good time to retire, if you know what I mean."

Jasper nodded. He knew, all right.

"The thing is, if this play for Malloy doesn't work out, I may not be hanging up my towel. If we can't nail him through legit means, I'll take him out any way I can."

"I wouldn't blame you. And for the record, we're not having this conversation."

"Didn't say a thing," Jasper said.

"And now I'm out of here. Wait until I'm off the property before you get naked. Would suck if I forgot something and had to come back."

"Funny man," Zelda said, then pulled off her shirt, leaving her only in her bra.

"What the hell?" Jasper asked, not sure if he was shocked or amused or horrified.

"I'm trying to hurry him on his way."

Ollie raised a brow. "For the record, if I didn't

know that Jasper would kick my ass, that might have the opposite effect."

Amusement lit her face, and Jasper watched as she held back laughter—and held her shirt to her chest.

As soon as Ollie was gone, she spun to face him. "Oh. My. God. I thought he was gay."

He fought to stifle his own laughter. "As far as I know, he's not. Jamie mentioned a fiancée a while back, and rumor has it he had a thing for Nikki before she ended up with Damien."

She groaned. "Well, I'm off my game. But Trevor's gay, right? I'm not off about that? And so they're just good friends?"

"That's what I heard."

She exhaled loudly. "Remind me to keep my clothes on when other people are around."

"I hope that's not something about which you really need a reminder." He stepped closer, then unhooked her bra. She shimmied out of it, then out of the sweatpants she'd changed into while he and Ollie had talked in the kitchen. Now she was standing before him naked, and as always, he had to wonder what he'd done to deserve her.

He took her hand. "Come here," he said, leading her to the couch.

She pulled a blanket onto her lap, but he pushed it away. Her brows rose. "If you're not giving me a blanket, you at least have to get naked with me."

"Believe me, that's on the agenda. But right now, I'm enjoying the view. And I wanted to talk to you." As he spoke, he took her hand, tracing idle patterns on her palm.

"Is something wrong?"

"No. Just he opposite. I just wanted tell you how desperately in love with you I am. In case you didn't already know"

He watched her face, the joy that filled it, and it humbled him more than he could imagine. She felt that for him. She'd chosen him.

Her smile was bright as sunshine, and she grinned as she moved her hand to the blanket, then very slowly and deliberately, pushed it off the couch.

"Now," she whispered. "Make love to me now."

Oh, yes.

He bent over her, his lips to hers, then down to her breasts, lower still so he could taste her. He explored her. Cherished her. *Worshipped* her. Every bit of skin, every soft place, every sweet secret. He knew her so intimately. She was in him, and he was in her.

Only when she couldn't take it anymore and writhed beneath him, begging him to fuck her, did he finally undress. They made love right there on the sofa, then again in the bedroom, a bottle of wine and two glasses on the side table.

When they were finally sated and a little bit drunk, they curled up together, limbs intertwined, and Jasper realized that the shift was finally complete. Sandra and Bonnie were still part of him, but now they were his past.

And Zelda was his present and all his days to come.

CHAPTER TWENTY-FOUR

"You're sure this is going to work?" Jasper asks. We are sitting in the back of a cargo van, and I'm rearranging my shirt, trying to get it to not be so incredibly uncomfortable. "I already asked you that," I remind him. "And you were right when you told me it would. I know my stepfather. He smells money, and he'll be here in an instant."

"This makes me nervous," he says.

"That's because you love me." I bend forward and give him a kiss. "It's good that you're nervous. But I promise you, this is a plan worthy of a Martin King novel."

He laughs. "That's what I'm worried about. Usually truth is stranger than fiction. I'm not sure what we're dealing with now that we're mixing both."

"All we're doing is making tar paper."

"A sticky trap for your stepfather. I just don't like that you are the glue."

We've been working on this plan for days, almost twenty-four/seven, our only breaks being late at night when we climb into bed together. It feels right and perfect having him beside me. It's not even about the sex, though that is a major perk; it's the way it feels, knowing that he's there and that he loves me.

We haven't talked about what we'll do after this operation, when we're no longer working round-the-clock and staying in the same house is no longer a boon for the operation.

Thankfully, my smart watch beeps before I get too lost in the weeds about our personal life.

I glance down to read the message from Brandon, one of the guys Matthew Holt recommended for this operation. Then I look up and flash a winning smile at Jasper. "Well," I say, "I guess it's time for my close-up."

I start to move toward the side door of the van, but he takes my wrist and pulls me back. The kiss is long and deep, and I melt into it, only pulling away when my watch buzzes again.

"Thanks to you, I probably have to reapply my lipstick."

He laughs, then kisses me again. "You're beautiful. Now go out there and don't get dead."

"That's the plan. Sort of."

He rolls his eyes, then moves to stay out of sight as I open the door and step down. I see Brandon about a block away, bobbing in a sea of tourists.

I've gotten out on Hollywood Boulevard, right along the Walk of Stars. I glance around to see if anyone has noticed me, but I don't see anything.

As far as I can tell, there's nothing at all unusual about me being here. And why should there be? Folks come to Hollywood Boulevard all the time.

I adjust my purse on my shoulder and start to stroll. I'm dressed in a loose skirt with a peasant-style top. It's white and flowy, but the undergarment is constricting as hell. I don't have a weapon on me, but theoretically, I have a whole battalion of undercover agents keeping an eye on me. I haven't spotted one of them.

I hope that's because they're good.

As far as we know, my stepfather is out of town with my mother, but I'm not going to feel safe ever until I know that he's gone. I felt uncomfortable enough when I believed he was a plain old asshole. Now that I know how diabolical he is, I want the man behind bars. Or dead. Either way works for me.

What's been an even worse pill to swallow is the intel that shows my mother wasn't just riding along as the sidepiece. She's been actively involved in all aspects of his operation. It's disconcerting, but also confirms my conviction that, biology aside, that woman is not my mother.

I hum a little bit, singing a happy tune as I think of their impending demise, and I walk down the street, scoping out the sites. As a general rule, I wouldn't come to Hollywood Boulevard. It's far too touristy. But it suits my purposes today, and it seemed like a better place for this particular project than Rodeo Drive or the Third Street Promenade.

Another block, and I'm still doing my window shopping. I glance at my watch, wondering if I have a message. There isn't one.

I turn around to look back and see if the van and Jasper are still in place. They are. I frown, wondering what's gone wrong.

When I turn back around to continue my walk, there's a man in front of me. He's wearing a black ball cap and dark sunglasses. He also has a gun aimed right at my chest.

I stumble backward, my heart pounding. "Oh God," I say. "Oh, God, what are you doing? Take whatever you want. Just don't hurt me."

"Your purse, bitch," he yells, and in my peripheral vision, I notice several tourists gawking. I want to call for help, but I can't. I just can't.

I pass him my purse, and he grabs it out of my hand.

Then he laughs, a cold, chilling laugh.

Next thing I know, he's pulled the trigger. I feel the shock of pain as the bullet impacts my chest.

I stumble, then fall. As I do, I see a man in jeans and a blue T-shirt tackle my assailant.

Down they go, and at the same time that my attacker hits the ground, my entire world goes dark.

CHAPTER TWENTY-FIVE

J asper waited in the classically decorated
lawyer's office with the well-dressed attorney
and two somewhat schlubby plainclothes
detectives. He paced in front of the sofa that dominated an inviting sitting area, presumably to calm
nervous clients.

He counted himself among that group. He'd
been waiting for this meeting since the shooting,
and he was very much on edge.

With a sigh, he dropped down onto the sofa
and leaned forward, then started rubbing his
temples. It was so odd that Zelda wasn't beside
him. Even a week after the shooting, it still seemed
surreal.

The press had gone crazy, of course. The
Hollywood Boulevard attack on a well-known
author and heiress. One of their own.

Some bystanders who managed to catch a few

pictures of that horrible event sold them to tabloids for a tidy sum. Others became social media stars, holding back the image sales in favor of likes and shares and trending on TikTok. Numerous articles were written, all trying to discern who the shooter had been. The police hadn't caught anyone. There was no criminal to prosecute, no one at whose feet the public could lay blame.

Or at least there hadn't been in the long days since the event itself.

Now, maybe that had changed.

Please, please, let that have changed. He wanted this to be over. He needed closure. Needed to know that everything he'd done in the interim since the shooting and the hours he'd been so alone hadn't been for nothing.

With a sigh, he stood and crossed the room to help himself to a cup of coffee. The attorney was still talking with the cops. It seemed like everyone in the room was on edge, aware that something important was happening. That something was about to change. That maybe, after today, Jasper would have his life back.

After what seemed like another eternity, but was only ten minutes, he heard a click, then a voice over the intercom. "Mr. Michelson, your eleven o'clock is here."

Jasper bent his head, letting his oversized jacket and black ball cap provide some camouflage. He was here to observe, at least at first. He didn't want to be recognized.

"The door opened, and Carter Malloy stepped inside, his well-dressed wife, Amelia, standing right beside him. They both walked with stiff posture, as if they were emulating royalty.

It took all of Jasper's effort, not to slap them. Malloy skimmed the room with those dark eyes that took in everything. The man was smart, no doubt about that. He'd accomplished a lot in his life. Perhaps too much. Perhaps he'd finally tipped the scales.

"Mr. Michelson," Malloy said. "We're so sorry it's taken us so long to get here. International travel is such a bear. But we are ready to settle our daughter's estate."

Mr. Michelson nodded and stepped forward. "It's a pleasure to meet you," he said. "Please have a seat."

Both Amelia and Malloy stepped more fully into the room. It was only then that Malloy noticed Jasper on the sofa, and Jasper dipped his head more deeply.

"I didn't realize you had another client," Malloy said.

"Oh no. This isn't a client. He'll be leaving soon. We just have one small bit of business to attend to before that."

"Well, this is highly irregular," Amelia said.

"After all, this is our time. And you should have respected our privacy."

"As you know," Mr. Michelson said, "I represent your daughter's estate, not you. And Mr. Kent is here to stand for your daughter."

"Excuse me?" Malloy said as Jasper clenched his fists at his sides, then slowly lifted his face.

He saw Malloy look at him. Blank at first, then something that might be recognition flared in his eyes. He took a step backwards, his eyes going from the lawyer to the two plainclothes detectives, still standing in the corner.

"What is this? What's going on?"

One of the detectives took a step forward. "Mr. Malloy, welcome back to the United States. You're under arrest for murder, conspiracy to murder, and other felony charges. You have the right to remain silent," he said, continuing to Mirandize the bastard as the second cop crossed to Amelia and arrested her as well.

"This is absurd," Malloy said, yanking back his hands as the officer tried to cuff him. A moment later, three more officers stepped in from a connecting office.

"We'd prefer not to have to restrain you," one of them said.

"We're here about our daughter's estate," Malloy snapped. "The poor girl has died, and you're playing foolish games.

"Oh, well that's where you're wrong," Jasper

said standing up. "These games aren't foolish. These games are called a sting. And thankfully, your daughter's very much alive."

He looked back to the door where the most recent police officers had entered from, and held his breath until Zelda stepped through.

She walked calmly at first, then hurried into his arms. They hadn't seen each other since the shooting, unwilling to risk the press getting a whiff of the truth.

Instead, she'd been staying in a secluded suite at the Stark Century, attended to only by Damien Stark's most trusted employees. "I've missed you," she said, hugging him tight.

"Don't you ever go away again," he said, only realizing after he'd spoken the real meaning of those words. He glanced at her face, unsure of her reaction, and was delighted to see her wide smile of absolute pleasure.

"You little bitch," Amelia said. "I'm your mother. I gave birth to you. I took care of you."

Zelda glanced blandly at her mother, then turned back to Jasper. "I'm absolutely starving. Do you want to go to lunch?"

"Yeah," he said. "Lunch would be terrific." They left the lawyer's office without a second look back, leaving Zelda's mother and stepfather alone with the cops to ponder their pitiful future.

CHAPTER TWENTY-SIX

"God, I've missed you," Jasper says as we tumble through the door to my hotel suite.

"That's my line," I retort, laughing as he starts to tug off my shirt. "Hey, I might need that."

"Trust me. You won't."

"Well, if you're certain," I say, then strip the rest of the way. He does the same, and we race each other to the bed, then collapse on it in a tumble of laughter and kisses that quickly turn heated.

"Jasper." I hear the need in my voice.

"I know," he says.

"I missed you so much. Nobody called or even sent me messages. I was so lonely." That had been protocol, just in case the few people who knew the truth were being watched. But I was the one who'd gotten the short end of the stick.

"I'll tell you everything," he promises. "But not now."

He doesn't even give me the chance to respond before he has me on my back. He kisses me, stroking my hair, my neck, my breasts. I hook my legs around his hips, then whisper, "Please."

That's all it takes. I'm so ready, and I arch up as he enters me, and we move together, our eyes open as if seeing each other for the first time.

"I love you," I whisper and see his response flare in his eyes, then feel it in his kiss. And then, just as I'm on the brink of a mind-blowing orgasm, I hear him whisper those words in my ear.

"I love you too, Zelda. You're mine."

As if the words are a trigger, I explode in his arms, flying up and up, past the ceiling and all the way to the stars.

When I come back to earth, I don't want to do anything except cuddle in his arms, and thankfully he feels the same.

"We do need to eat. Are you comfortable going out?"

"Ryan thinks I should wait until after the screening. We don't know if Malloy planned something. If so, there may still be snipers for me."

He nods. "I know. We have teams investigating. So far no whispers, but we're on it." He cups my cheek. "I want you safe, but I hate you being hostage."

"It's not much longer. And considering Malloy's people—if there are any—probably know your role, you should probably stay here, too."

"Trapped with you for a few more days? How will I stand it?"

I laugh, then straddle him. "I'm sure we'll think of something."

"And your security? Nothing dicey happen?"

"Nope. I ordered room service, read, and watched a lot of TV."

"That sounds like a plan for the evening," he says. "Except instead of watching TV, we can play catchup."

Since neither of us are hungry yet, we slide back under the covers, stretched out on our sides facing each other. "Have you learned anything more?"

"A little," he tells me. "Quincy and I did some poking around. There's no doubt that your stepfather really was The Maestro, so we did the world a service taking him down."

"I always knew I hated that man, and for more than just being an ass."

"He used his diplomatic connections to run some pretty nasty enterprises, which we can talk about in more detail when we're not naked."

I laugh. "Fair enough. What else?"

"I finished *Intercontinental*. And the next one. My girlfriend knows how to write a thriller."

"Yeah?" My smile is painfully wide. I hadn't realized until this moment just how much I wanted his approval. "I'm glad you liked it. You remind me of King."

"Must be why you love me," he says, making me laugh. Though he's probably not wrong.

"Oh," he adds. "We found a motive."

I lean back. "Really? For Sandra and Bonnie?"

He nods, his expression heavy with sadness. "I killed a mole about fifteen years ago on a mission. Apparently, he was The Maestro's most reliable and trusted source for black market intel. I didn't know, as that wasn't my mission."

"It was about payback." I stroke his cheek. "I'm so, so sorry."

"I know. Me too. But the closure helps. At least I have an answer."

"And it turns out Sandra and Bonnie were right," I say. "The truth was hiding in plain sight all along."

I bend over to kiss him. "I know it's cold comfort, but at least you have some answers."

"It helps," he agrees. "And I have you, too."

"You do," I say. "Forever."

He takes my hand and kisses my fingertips. "Forever," he repeats.

I sigh happily. "I love you. And I'm hungry. I'm going to grab my robe, then I'm going to read the menu, then I'm going to order us a buffet."

He laughs. "I could eat."

I practically dance to the closet, then start to pull it open. I pause to turn back and ask Jasper if he wants a dessert when I'm yanked off my feet and into a strong pair of arms.

"Lovely to see you again," Owen says. "And how special that you'll die in your birthday suit."

"You fucker," I hiss, my heart pounding with so much fear I'm surprised it doesn't break a rib. "You really are evil."

"Me? Your boyfriend's the one who's destroyed my mentor. But I'll destroy him." He bends down and stage whispers in my ear, loud enough for Jasper to hear, "I'll destroy him by destroying you."

I can't breath. I'm terrified that this time it really is the end. Owen has a knife in his hand, and I'm confident he'll use it.

Then I see Jasper, and my fear evaporates. "It's okay, baby," he says, shifting on the bed. "We're just going to do what Owen says. He's in charge, right?"

"Right," I say, getting ready. I keep my eyes on him, and the moment I see him thrust his hand between the mattress and the headboard, I jerk hard to the right, wrenching myself from Owen's grasp.

I drop to the floor even as the crack of the gun echoes through the room. I hear a thud, then roll over to find Owen on the floor, a bullet through the brain and the knife clenched in his hand.

"You knew," I say, climbing to my feet and racing to the bed and into his arms.

"Of course, I knew. I checked the second I got on the bed. I figured it would be there. After all, in every hotel, King hides his spare gun between the mattress and the headboard. And there's always one last bad guy at the end."

EPILOGUE

I stand in the theater lobby basking in the circle of Jasper's arms. The gala trailer reveal is going great, but most of all I'm having a fabulous time with my friends and my fiancé. Fast, maybe, but we both know it's right.

Owen is dead, my mom and stepfather are incarcerated, and no less than three teams from three different agencies have determined that there is no outstanding threat to me. I hope they're right —it would suck to get gunned down at my own gala.

I tell Jasper that, and he rolls his eyes. "My fiancée is into gallows humor," he says, then nuzzles my neck and makes me giggle.

"You two are just too happy," Ollie says, then shakes Jasper's hand. I see Trevor across the room and wave to him. He's by himself, and he smiles as he approaches us. "Hey. Congratulations. That is going to be one really kick ass movie."

"I know," I say still giddy. He reaches out and brushes Ollie's shoulder. "Good to see you again."

"You too," Ollie says. "Listen my date stood me up. I'm about to go grab a drink. Want to come?"

Trevor practically lights up as he agrees, and the two promise to circle back. "Do you think Ollie realizes?"

Jasper considers. "I hope so. They look good together. And I'd hate to see a misunderstanding screw a friendship."

Simon comes over to give me a hug and congratulate me for being freed from my hotel prison. "I'm heading out," he says.

"You're not staying for the actual movie? Damien got us such great seats."

"Mine is in the same box as Francesca Murratti." He shakes his head. "Not happening."

"You *really* don't do Hollywood."

"I like to think of it as an allergy." He gives me a quick kiss on the cheek, then heads off, telling us he's hurrying before someone catches him and drags him back in.

"I don't think he realizes what a large percent of the SSA client list has Hollywood connections," Jasper says.

I bite back a laugh. "Wouldn't it be funny if he got assigned to protect some Hollywood big wig."

"Might happen," he says. "I overheard

Francesca talking to Damien earlier. I think she was talking about hiring him. And I thought I heard him mention Simon's name."

"Oh, my," I say, trying to stifle my laughter.

"He'll never survive," Jasper says, grinning as he hooks his arm through mine. "Come on. Let's go find our friends and watch this movie."

"And snuggle in the dark," I add.

"That, wife-to-be, goes without saying." Then he kisses me, and we walk forward toward our friends together.

MORE STARK SECURITY!

Want a bit more of Jasper? Keep reading for the bonus prequel!

After that, enjoy an excerpt from *Release Me*, the runaway bestseller that is first book in Nikki & Damien Stark's romance!

Finally, be sure not to miss Simon and Francesca in *Charmed By You*, followed by Ollie and Trevor's romance in *Tangled With You*.

HIDDEN WITH YOU BONUS PREQUEL

The woman at the roulette table was stunning, no doubt about that. Blonde waves framed a face highlighted by intelligent eyes and a strong jaw. A woman in her early thirties who looked like she knew what she wanted and expected to get it. A cold woman without doubts or insecurities.

Once upon a time, she'd have been exactly his type. The kind of woman he'd pick up in a bar, then tumble into a bed. But that was back when he'd been younger and stupider. Back before he'd married Sandra and they'd had Bonnie and his whole life had changed. Back when he still gave a shit.

Stop it.

Former MI6 agent Jasper Kent glanced at the photo in his hand. A faded print at least a decade old, the image of a girl in her late teens or early twenties. Jeans and a T-shirt, her expression a little lost. Nothing like the confident woman in the casino. But it was her; Jasper was certain of it.

The woman in the picture was the woman who'd just bet five hundred quid on red 32. His source.

Perhaps even his target.

He wasn't sure. Not yet. He'd received the photo ten months ago, posted from Oxford with no return address and no letter. The only thing in the plain brown envelope had been the photo and the simple words written in plain block letters in silver marker on the back: *Find her. She knows.*

He'd set out eagerly to track the mysterious woman down, but as each day failed to move him closer to the goal, he'd become more and more frustrated. He'd never quit, though. And this week all of the hours he'd invested had paid off.

He'd found her. *Melinda Barrett.* And that meant he was that much closer to avenging Sandra and Bonnie.

At the table, the ball quit spinning, finally settling into a slot with a definitive *plonk.* "Black 15," the croupier said. "Madame loses."

Her mouth curved into a smile as she slid him a hundred quid chip as a tip. "Ah, well, this isn't the first time, and it won't be the last." She slid off her stool, straightened her skirt, and headed toward the lounge in the back of the elegant room.

Jasper rolled his neck, releasing the tension, then straightened his jacket, relishing the pressure of the blade holstered under the tailored wool and silk blend.

He pushed away from the wall and fell in step behind her, far enough away that he could blend into the well-dressed crowd. They passed blackjack tables, slot machines, and a craps table before she finally pushed through the etched glass doors and into the elegant room adorned with polished wood and crystal chandeliers. By the time he did the same, she already sat perched on a stool at the bar, her polished fingernails tapping as she waited for the bartender to take her order.

Jasper took the seat beside her, lifted his hand, and caught Mike's attention. "Two martinis," he said, then caught her eye. "Unless you'd prefer something else?"

Her head tilted slightly as she studied him. He saw the flare of heat in her eyes, and allowed himself a silent congratulation. "A martini sounds lovely. Thank you."

"It's my pleasure. A martini seems a small price to pay for the privilege of sitting next to a beautiful woman."

She laughed. "Now you're pushing it."

He offered her a smile. "Just testing boundaries."

"I like genuine men."

He nodded. "I'm very glad to hear it. I'm Jazz by the way," he said, offering her his little-used nickname.

Her phone buzzed, and she tapped the screen. He noted the initials that popped up—*S.C.*

They meant nothing to him, and yet Jasper couldn't help but wonder if S.C. had mailed him the photo. If one of her friends or colleagues had held onto the secret all these years and had only recently decide to help Jasper by betraying this woman.

"I'm Melinda," she said, silencing the phone. A text notification flashed on the lock screen. Also from SC, though no actual message was displayed. She frowned. "I'm so sorry. Could you excuse me for a moment. My sister. I need to call her back."

"Of course. Take your time."

She was already off the stool and heading to the back of the lounge.

"We'll be back," he said as the bartender delivered their drinks.

"Of course, sir."

He slid off the stool, then followed in Melinda's wake to an oak-paneled hallway lined with a series of small, private restrooms. She must have stepped into one, and he glanced around, seeing only one with a red *occupied* indicator. He stood in front of it, patiently waiting as he considered his options. The lock clicked, the red indicator flipped to a green *vacant*, and the door pulled open.

He didn't think, just slammed through the door and pushed his target against the wall, his hand at her throat. "Lie to me, and I swear I will kill you."

"Who are you?" She trembled beneath his hand, her eyes full of fear. "Please. Please don't hurt me. Just tell me what you want. Anything. Please. Anything you want."

Tears streamed down her cheeks, and he told himself not to waiver. She'd been involved. She *knew*. She wasn't some terrified innocent. She was the one who doled out the terror. Or who stood by and let it happen. Or who kept silent afterwards, just as guilty as whoever had wielded the knife that had killed his wife and daughter.

"Ten years ago. A woman. A little girl." His voice trembled and he squared his shoulders, forcing his words out. "Did you kill them?"

"I don't—I don't know what you're talking about."

"Don't lie." He moved with lightning speed, retrieving his knife with his left hand, then replacing his hand at her throat with the blade. "Don't you dare fucking lie to me."

She said nothing, but her eyes were wide, her breath shaky.

"My wife, Sandra. My five-year-old daughter, Bonnie. And a knife very much like this one."

"I didn't... it wasn't me. I don't know—"

"Yes, you fucking do." With his free hand, he pulled out the photo. Showed her the image of herself. Showed her the four words on the back. *Find her. She knows.* "I found you," he said. "Melinda James Grady. An ice-cold bitch. Married

to Franklin Grady, an eighty-two year old multi-millionaire who died just one year later and left her a fortune. Did you kill him, too? Just like you killed my family?"

"No! I didn't! I wouldn't! Franklin was good to me. And I didn't know. Please, I'm sorry about your family, but I didn't know. I didn't know."

She was trembling now, her words clogged with tears. Gone was the confident woman he'd watched at the roulette table. This was the girl in the photo again, a little lost, and very, very scared.

"I believe you," he said. "You didn't know. But you do now. Tell me, Melinda. Tell me who killed them."

"I don't know."

"Do not fuck with me." He lifted the blade so that she could feel the cool steel beneath her chin.

"I don't, I don't, I swear. There was a man. When I was a teen. He—he took care of me in exchange for...." She trailed off, closing her eyes as she drew in a breath. When she opened them again, he saw a hint of the woman from the roulette table. Stronger. A fighter.

"Go on."

"I was a runaway. He took care of me, and sex was his payment."

"He killed my family? What's his name?"

"Tarlton Raleigh, but he didn't kill them."

His eyes narrowed as he studied her. So far, he thought she was telling the truth. "Go on."

"Mr. Raleigh did bookkeeping work for a man they called the Maestro. Hid money. That kind of thing."

"The Maestro?"

She nodded, the tiniest movement of her head above the blade. "Because he could play out pain like a symphony." A single tear trickled down her cheek. "Mr. Raleigh gave me to him for a night. The Maestro said he needed a girl. That he needed to take the edge off. He—I—I mean, Mr. Raleigh sent me."

Jasper went cold inside, and he had to force himself not to take the blade away. This could all be bullshit.

"He—well, I understood his nickname after that night. It was...." She trailed off with a shudder, silent tears flowing freely now.

"My family," he prompted.

"Later," she said. "I learned later that was what he'd done before. Why he needed to ... needed me to ... why he used me."

Jasper felt his shoulders relax. "It's okay," he said gently, pulling the knife away. "I get it."

"I don't know how to help you. I wish I could. Truly. But I don't know where to find him."

"What about Mr. Raleigh? Can you find him?"

She shook her head. "He's long gone. I heard he's in California now. He always said he wanted to live in Beverly Hills. But that's all I know. I swear, I haven't spoken to him in years. And I try not to think about either of them. I—I married Franklin because he was kind. He didn't want to touch me. We talked. We were friends. He was kind."

He took a step back, not wanting to feel sorry for this woman. He needed to stay cold. To stay focused on his mission.

He drew a breath, willing ice to flow in his veins. It didn't work. With a sigh, he plucked a tissue from a silver box. He held it out for her.

"Thank you," she said.

He didn't answer. He just turned and walked out of the small restroom. Then he strode to the bar, put down a fifty-pound note, and kept on walking.

When he reached the street, he pulled out his phone, dialed, and was pleasantly surprised when he heard his friend rather than a voicemail message.

"Jasper Kent, I'm completely gobsmacked." Quincy Radcliffe's voice sounded sharp and clear on the line, despite being all the way in Los Angeles. "What the devil are you up to these days? I heard you'd left Her Majesty's service, too."

"Free agent for a few years now. Just like you, old man." Jasper caught himself smiling. He and Quince had worked a few MI6 missions together, and he'd forgotten how much he enjoyed the ex-agent's company.

"Are you in town? Is this a social call?"

"Not yet, and not really."

"You're going to have to translate that for me."

"I'm not in the States yet, but I'm thinking of following in your footsteps. Moving to the land of sunshine and movie stars."

Quince chuckled. "I see far fewer movie stars than you'd think. But the sunshine is as advertised. But I didn't think you'd ever leave London. At least not until you found—*Oh, bloody hell.* Did you find their killer?"

Jasper released a long, slow breath. "I'm moving on, Quince," he said, telling himself the words weren't a lie. "It's time for me to move on."

"I'm sorry, mate. But I think you're making the right decision. You're retiring?"

"No. I'll stay in the game."

"I know you've been working freelance, but if you're looking for steady work, I could probably get you on here at Stark Security."

Jasper wasn't entirely sure he qualified as a good man, and he hadn't been a team player in years. He had no intention of telling anyone he was searching for the Maestro, but Stark Security had acquired a solid reputation. With the resources of billionaire Damien Stark backing the security firm, Jasper would have access to the kinds of databases that could pinpoint the Maestro in weeks, not years.

"So are you interested?"

The question lingered as Jasper imagined finally avenging his wife and daughter, gone now for ten long years. He thought of Sandra's sweet smile. Of Bonnie's delightful giggle. They'd been love and laughter and joy, and the Maestro had taken that away. Had taken *them* away.

Jasper knew he'd never find another woman to love. That he didn't want another family. He was damaged goods. Broken. And alone suited him just fine.

But he wasn't done yet. They deserved to be avenged, and he craved that closure.

Hell, he craved revenge.

He drew in a breath, then let it out slowly as he pictured the Maestro's dead body. Finally, he allowed himself a slow, cold smile.

"Yes," he told Quincy. "I'm interested. I'm very interested."

RELEASE ME EXCERPT

1

A cool ocean breeze caresses my bare shoulders, and I shiver, wishing I'd taken my roommate's advice and brought a shawl with me tonight. I arrived in Los Angeles only four days ago, and I haven't yet adjusted to the concept of summer temperatures changing with the setting of the sun. In Dallas, June is hot, July is hotter, and August is hell.

Not so in California, at least not by the beach. LA Lesson Number One: Always carry a sweater if you'll be out after dark.

Of course, I could leave the balcony and go back inside to the party. Mingle with the millionaires. Chat up the celebrities. Gaze dutifully at the paintings. It is a gala art opening, after all, and my boss brought me here to meet and greet and charm and chat. Not to lust over the panorama that is coming alive in front of me. Bloodred clouds bursting against the pale orange sky. Blue-gray waves shimmering with dappled gold.

I press my hands against the balcony rail and lean forward, drawn to the intense, unreachable beauty of the setting sun. I regret that I didn't bring the battered Nikon I've had since high school. Not that it would have fit in my itty-bitty beaded purse. And a bulky camera bag paired with a little black dress is a big, fat fashion no-no.

But this is my very first Pacific Ocean sunset, and I'm determined to document the moment. I pull out my iPhone and snap a picture.

"Almost makes the paintings inside seem redundant, doesn't it?" I recognize the throaty, feminine voice and turn to face Evelyn Dodge, retired actress turned agent turned patron of the arts—and my hostess for the evening.

"I'm so sorry. I know I must look like a giddy tourist, but we don't have sunsets like this in Dallas."

"Don't apologize," she says. "I pay for that view every month when I write the mortgage check. It damn well better be spectacular."

I laugh, immediately more at ease.

"Hiding out?"

"Excuse me?"

"You're Carl's new assistant, right?" she asks, referring to my boss of three days.

"Nikki Fairchild."

"I remember now. Nikki from Texas." She looks me up and down, and I wonder if she's disappointed that I don't have big hair and cowboy boots. "So who does he want you to charm?"

"Charm?" I repeat, as if I don't know exactly what she means.

She cocks a single brow. "Honey, the man would rather walk on burning coals than come to an art show. He's fishing for investors and you're the bait." She makes a rough noise in the back of her throat. "Don't worry. I won't press you to tell me who. And I don't blame you for hiding out. Carl's brilliant, but he's a bit of a prick."

"It's the brilliant part I signed on for," I say, and she barks out a laugh.

The truth is that she's right about me being the bait. "Wear a cocktail dress," Carl had said. "Something flirty."

Seriously? I mean, *Seriously?*

I should have told him to wear his own damn cocktail dress. But I didn't. Because I want this job. I fought to get this job. Carl's company, C-Squared Technologies, successfully launched three web-based products in the last eighteen months. That track record had caught the industry's eye, and Carl had been hailed as a man to watch.

More important from my perspective, that meant he was a man to learn from, and I'd prepared for the job interview with an intensity bordering on obsession. Landing the position had been a huge coup for me. So what if he wanted me to wear something flirty? It was a small price to pay.

Shit.

"I need to get back to being the bait," I say.

"Oh, hell. Now I've gone and made you feel either guilty or self-conscious. Don't be. Let them get liquored up in there first. You catch more flies with alcohol anyway. Trust me. I know."

She's holding a pack of cigarettes, and now she taps one out, then extends the pack to me. I shake my head. I love the smell of tobacco—it reminds me of my grandfather—but actually inhaling the smoke does nothing for me.

"I'm too old and set in my ways to quit," she says. "But God forbid I smoke in my own damn house. I swear, the mob would burn me in effigy. You're not going to start lecturing me on the dangers of secondhand smoke, are you?"

"No," I promise.

"Then how about a light?"

I hold up the itty-bitty purse. "One lipstick, a credit card, my driver's license, and my phone."

"No condom?"

"I didn't think it was that kind of party," I say dryly.

"I knew I liked you." She glances around the balcony. "What the hell kind of party am I throwing if I don't even have one goddamn candle on one goddamn table? Well, fuck it." She puts the unlit cigarette to her mouth and inhales, her eyes closed and her expression rapturous. I can't help but like her. She wears hardly any makeup, in stark contrast to all the other women here tonight, myself included, and her dress is more of a caftan, the batik pattern as interesting as the woman herself.

She's what my mother would call a brassy broad—loud, large, opinionated, and self-confident. My mother would hate her. I think she's awesome.

She drops the unlit cigarette onto the tile and grinds it with the toe of her shoe. Then she signals to one of the catering staff, a girl dressed all in black and carrying a tray of champagne glasses.

The girl fumbles for a minute with the sliding door that opens onto the balcony, and I imagine those flutes tumbling off, breaking against the hard tile, the scattered shards glittering like a wash of diamonds.

I picture myself bending to snatch up a broken stem. I see the raw edge cutting into the soft flesh at the base of my thumb as I squeeze. I watch myself clutching it tighter, drawing strength from the pain, the way some people might try to extract luck from a rabbit's foot.

The fantasy blurs with memory, jarring me with its potency. It's fast and powerful, and a little disturbing because I haven't needed the pain in a long time, and I don't understand why I'm thinking about it now, when I feel steady and in control.

I am fine, I think. *I am fine, I am fine, I am fine.*

"Take one, honey," Evelyn says easily, holding a flute out to me.

I hesitate, searching her face for signs that my mask has slipped and she's caught a glimpse of my rawness. But her face is clear and genial.

"No, don't you argue," she adds, misinterpreting my hesitation. "I bought a dozen cases and I hate to see good alcohol go to waste. Hell no," she adds when the girl tries to hand her a flute. "I hate the stuff. Get me a vodka. Straight up. Chilled. Four olives. Hurry up, now. Do you want me to dry up like a leaf and float away?"

The girl shakes her head, looking a bit like a twitchy, frightened rabbit. Possibly one that had sacrificed his foot for someone else's good luck.

Evelyn's attention returns to me. "So how do you like LA? What have you seen? Where have you been? Have you bought a map of the stars yet? Dear God, tell me you're not getting sucked into all that tourist bullshit."

"Mostly I've seen miles of freeway and the inside of my apartment."

"Well, that's just sad. Makes me even more glad that Carl dragged your skinny ass all the way out here tonight."

I've put on fifteen welcome pounds since the years when my mother monitored every tiny thing that went in my mouth, and while I'm perfectly happy with my size-eight ass, I wouldn't describe it as skinny. I know Evelyn means it as a compliment, though, and so I smile. "I'm glad he brought me, too. The paintings really are amazing."

"Now don't do that—don't you go sliding into the polite-conversation routine. No, no," she says before I can protest. "I'm sure you mean it. Hell, the paintings are wonderful. But you're getting the flat-eyed look of a girl on her best behavior, and we can't have that. Not when I was getting to know the real you."

"Sorry," I say. "I swear I'm not fading away on you."

Because I genuinely like her, I don't tell her that she's wrong—she hasn't met the real Nikki Fairchild. She's met Social Nikki who, much like Malibu Barbie, comes with a complete set of accessories. In my case, it's not a bikini and a convertible. Instead, I have the *Elizabeth Fairchild Guide for Social Gatherings.*

My mother's big on rules. She claims it's her Southern upbringing. In my weaker moments, I agree. Mostly, I just think she's a controlling bitch. Since the first time she took me for tea at the Mansion at Turtle Creek in Dallas at age three, I have had the rules drilled into my head. How to walk, how to talk, how to dress. What to eat, how much to drink, what kinds of jokes to tell.

I have it all down, every trick, every nuance, and I wear my practiced pageant smile like armor against the world. The result being that I don't think I could truly be myself at a party even if my life depended on it.

This, however, is not something Evelyn needs to know.

"Where exactly are you living?" she asks.

"Studio City. I'm sharing a condo with my best friend from high school."

"Straight down the 101 for work and then back home again. No wonder you've only seen concrete. Didn't anyone tell you that you should have taken an apartment on the Westside?"

"Too pricey to go it alone," I admit, and I can tell that my admission surprises her. When I make the effort—like when I'm Social Nikki—I can't help but look like I come from money. Probably because I do. Come from it, that is. But that doesn't mean I brought it with me.

"How old are you?"

"Twenty-four."

Evelyn nods sagely, as if my age reveals some secret about me. "You'll be wanting a place of your own soon enough. You call me when you do and we'll find you someplace with a view. Not as good as this one, of course, but we can manage something better than a freeway on-ramp."

"It's not that bad, I promise."

"Of course it's not," she says in a tone that says the exact opposite. "As for views," she continues, gesturing toward the now-dark ocean and the sky that's starting to bloom with stars, "you're welcome to come back anytime and share mine."

"I might take you up on that," I admit. "I'd love to bring a decent camera back here and take a shot or two."

"It's an open invitation. I'll provide the wine and you can provide the entertainment. A young woman loose in the city. Will it be a drama? A rom-com? Not a tragedy, I hope. I love a good cry as much as the next woman, but I like you. You need a happy ending."

I tense, but Evelyn doesn't know she's hit a nerve. That's why I moved to LA, after all. New life. New story. New Nikki.

I ramp up the Social Nikki smile and lift my champagne flute. "To happy endings. And to this amazing party. I think I've kept you from it long enough."

"Bullshit," she says. "I'm the one monopolizing you, and we both know it."

We slip back inside, the buzz of alcohol-fueled conversation replacing the soft calm of the ocean.

"The truth is, I'm a terrible hostess. I do what I want, talk to whoever I want, and if my guests feel slighted they can damn well deal with it."

I gape. I can almost hear my mother's cries of horror all the way from Dallas.

"Besides," she continues, "this party isn't supposed to be about me. I put together this little shindig to introduce Blaine and his art to the community. He's the one who should be doing the mingling, not me. I may be fucking him, but I'm not going to baby him."

Evelyn has completely destroyed my image of how a hostess for the not-to-be-missed social event of the weekend is supposed to behave, and I think I'm a little in love with her for that.

"I haven't met Blaine yet. That's him, right?" I point to a tall reed of a man. He is bald, but sports a red goatee. I'm pretty sure it's not his natural color. A small crowd hums around him, like bees drawing nectar from a flower. His outfit is certainly as bright as one.

"That's my little center of attention, all right," Evelyn says. "The man of the hour. Talented, isn't he?" Her hand sweeps out to indicate her massive living room. Every wall is covered with paintings. Except for a few benches, whatever furniture was once in the room has been removed and replaced with easels on which more paintings stand.

I suppose technically they are portraits. The models are nudes, but these aren't like anything you would see in a classical art book. There's something edgy about them. Something provocative and raw. I can tell that they are expertly conceived and carried out, and yet they disturb me, as if they reveal more about the person viewing the portrait than about the painter or the model.

As far as I can tell, I'm the only one with that

reaction. Certainly the crowd around Blaine is glowing. I can hear the gushing praise from here.

"I picked a winner with that one," Evelyn says. "But let's see. Who do you want to meet? Rip Carrington and Lyle Tarpin? Those two are guaranteed drama, that's for damn sure, and your roommate will be jealous as hell if you chat them up."

"She will?"

Evelyn's brows arch up. "Rip and Lyle? They've been feuding for weeks." She narrows her eyes at me. "The fiasco about the new season of their sitcom? It's all over the Internet? You really don't know them?"

"Sorry," I say, feeling the need to apologize. "My school schedule was pretty intense. And I'm sure you can imagine what working for Carl is like."

Speaking of …

I glance around, but I don't see my boss anywhere.

"That is one serious gap in your education," Evelyn says. "Culture—and yes, pop culture counts —is just as important as—what did you say you studied?"

"I don't think I mentioned it. But I have a double major in electrical engineering and computer science."

"So you've got brains and beauty. See? That's something else we have in common. Gotta say, though, with an education like that, I don't see why you signed up to be Carl's secretary."

I laugh. "I'm not, I swear. Carl was looking for someone with tech experience to work with him on the business side of things, and I was looking for a job where I could learn the business side. Get my feet wet. I think he was a little hesitant to hire me at first—my skills definitely lean toward tech—but I convinced him I'm a fast learner."

She peers at me. "I smell ambition."

I lift a shoulder in a casual shrug. "It's Los Angeles. Isn't that what this town is all about?"

"Ha! Carl's lucky he's got you. It'll be interesting to see how long he keeps you. But let's see ... who here would intrigue you ...?"

She casts about the room, finally pointing to a fifty-something man holding court in a corner. "That's Charles Maynard," she says. "I've known Charlie for years. Intimidating as hell until you get to know him. But it's worth it. His clients are either celebrities with name recognition or power brokers with more money than God. Either way, he's got all the best stories."

"He's a lawyer?"

"With Bender, Twain & McGuire. Very prestigious firm."

"I know," I say, happy to show that I'm not entirely ignorant, despite not knowing Rip or Lyle. "One of my closest friends works for the firm. He started here but he's in their New York office now."

"Well, come on, then, Texas. I'll introduce you." We take one step in that direction, but then Evelyn stops me. Maynard has pulled out his phone, and is shouting instructions at someone. I catch a few well-placed curses and eye Evelyn sideways. She looks unconcerned "He's a pussycat at heart. Trust me, I've worked with him before. Back in my agenting days, we put together more celebrity biopic deals for our clients than I can count. And we fought to keep a few tell-alls off the screen, too." She shakes her head, as if reliving those glory days, then pats my arm. "Still, we'll wait 'til he calms down a bit. In the meantime, though …"

She trails off, and the corners of her mouth turn down in a frown as she scans the room again. "I don't think he's here yet, but—oh! Yes! Now *there's* someone you should meet. And if you want to talk views, the house he's building has one that makes my view look like, well, like yours." She points toward the entrance hall, but all I see are bobbing heads and haute couture. "He hardly ever accepts invitations, but we go way back," she says.

I still can't see who she's talking about, but then the crowd parts and I see the man in profile. Goose bumps rise on my arms, but I'm not cold. In fact, I'm suddenly very, very warm.

He's tall and so handsome that the word is almost an insult. But it's more than that. It's not his looks, it's his *presence*. He commands the room simply by being in it, and I realize that Evelyn and I aren't the only ones looking at him. The entire crowd has noticed his arrival. He must feel the weight of all those eyes, and yet the attention doesn't faze him at all. He smiles at the girl with the champagne, takes a glass, and begins to chat casually with a woman who approaches him, a simpering smile stretched across her face.

"Damn that girl," Evelyn says. "She never did bring me my vodka."

But I barely hear her. "Damien Stark," I say. My voice surprises me. It's little more than breath.

Evelyn's brows rise so high I notice the movement in my peripheral vision. "Well, how about that?" she says knowingly. "Looks like I guessed right."

"You did," I admit. "Mr. Stark is just the man I want to see."

2

"Damien Stark is the holy grail." That's what Carl told me earlier that evening. Right after "Damn, Nikki. You look hot."

I think he was expecting me to blush and smile and thank him for his kind words. When I didn't, he cleared his throat and got down to business. "You know who Stark is, right?"

"You saw my resume," I reminded him. "The fellowship?" I'd been the recipient of the Stark

International Science Fellowship for four of my five years at the University of Texas, and those extra dollars every semester had made all the difference in the world to me. Of course, even without a fellowship, you'd have to be from Mars not to know about the man. Only thirty years old, the reclusive former tennis star had taken the millions he'd earned in prizes and endorsements and reinvented himself. His tennis days had been overshadowed by his new identity as an entrepreneur, and Stark's massive empire raked in billions every year.

"Right, right," Carl said, distracted. "Team April is presenting at Stark Applied Technology on Tuesday." At C-Squared, every product team is named after a month. With only twenty-three employees, though, the company has yet to tap into autumn or winter.

"That's fabulous," I said, and I meant it. Inventors, software developers, and eager new business owners practically wet themselves to get an interview with Damien Stark. That Carl had snagged just such an appointment was proof that my hoop-jumping to get this job had been worth it.

"Damn straight," Carl said. "We're showing off the beta version of the 3-D training software. Brian and Dave are on point with me," he added, referring to the two software developers who'd written most of the code for the product. Considering its applications in athletics and Stark Applied Technology's focus on athletic medicine and training, I had to guess that Carl was about to pitch another winner. "I want you at the meeting with us," he added, and I managed not to embarrass myself by doing a fist-pump in the air. "Right now, we're scheduled to meet with Preston Rhodes. Do you know who he is?"

"No."

"Nobody does. Because Rhodes *is* a nobody."

So Carl didn't have a meeting with Stark, after all. I, however, had a feeling I knew where this conversation was going.

"Pop quiz, Nikki. How does an up-and-coming genius like me get an in-person meeting with a powerhouse like Damien Stark?"

"Networking," I said. I wasn't an A-student for nothing.

"And that's why I hired you." He tapped his temple, even as his eyes roamed over my dress and lingered at my cleavage. At least he wasn't so gauche as to actually articulate the basic fact that he was hoping that my tits—rather than his product —would intrigue Stark enough that he'd attend the meeting personally. But honestly, I wasn't sure my girls were up to the task. I'm easy on the eyes, but I'm more the girl-next-door, America's-sweetheart type. And I happen to know that Stark goes for the runway supermodel type.

I learned that six years ago when he was still playing tennis and I was still chasing tiaras. He'd been the token celebrity judge at the Miss Tri-

County Texas pageant, and though we'd barely exchanged a dozen words at the mid-pageant reception, the encounter was burned into my memory.

I'd parked myself near the buffet and was contemplating the tiny squares of cheesecake, wondering if my mother would smell it on my breath if I ate just one, when he walked up with the kind of bold self-assurance that can seem like arrogance on some men, but on Damien Stark it just seemed sexy as hell. He eyed me first, then the cheesecakes. Then he took two and popped them both in his mouth. He chewed, swallowed, then grinned at me. His unusual eyes, one amber and one almost completely black, seemed to dance with mirth.

I tried to come up with something clever to say and failed miserably. So I just stood there, my polite smile plastered across my face as I wondered if his kiss would give me all the taste and none of the calories.

Then he leaned closer, and my breath hitched as his proximity increased. "I think we're kindred spirits, Miss Fairchild."

"I'm sorry?" Was he talking about the cheesecake? Good God, I hadn't actually looked jealous when he'd eaten them, had I? The idea was appalling.

"Neither of us wants to be here," he explained. He tilted his head slightly toward a nearby emergency exit, and I was overcome by the sudden image of him grabbing my hand and taking off running. The clarity of the thought alarmed me. But the certainty that I'd go with him didn't scare me at all.

"I—oh," I mumbled.

His eyes crinkled with his smile, and he opened his mouth to speak. I didn't learn what he had to say, though, because Carmela D'Amato swept over to join us, then linked her arm with his. "Damie, darling." Her Italian accent was as thick as her dark wavy hair. "Come. We should go, yes?" I've never been a big tabloid reader, but it's hard to avoid celebrity gossip when you're doing the pageant thing. So I'd seen the headlines and articles that paired the big-shot tennis star with the Italian supermodel.

"Miss Fairchild," he said with a parting nod, then turned to escort Carmela into the crowd and out of the building. I watched them leave, consoling myself with the thought that there was regret in his eyes as we parted ways. Regret and resignation.

There wasn't, of course. Why would there be? But that nice little fantasy got me through the rest of the pageant.

And I didn't say one word about the encounter to Carl. Some things are best played close to the vest. Including how much I'm looking forward to meeting Damien Stark again.

"Come on, Texas," Evelyn says, pulling me from my thoughts. "Let's go say howdy."

I feel a tap on my shoulder and turn to find Carl behind me. He sports the kind of grin that suggests he just got laid. I know better. He's just giddy with the anticipation of getting close to Damien Stark.

Well, me, too.

The crowd has shifted again, blocking my view of the man. I still haven't seen his face, just his profile, and now I can't even see that. Evelyn's leading the way, making forward progress through the crowd despite a few stops and starts to chat with her guests. We're on the move again when a barrel-chested man in a plaid sport coat shifts to the left, once again revealing Damien Stark.

He is even more magnificent now than he was six years ago. The brashness of youth has been replaced by a mature confidence. He is Jason and Hercules and Perseus—a figure so strong and beautiful and heroic that the blood of the gods must flow through him, because how else could a being so fine exist in this world? His face consists of hard lines and angles that seem sculpted by light and shadows, making him appear both classically gorgeous and undeniably unique. His dark hair absorbs the light as completely as a raven's wing, but it is not nearly as smooth. Instead, it looks wind-tossed, as if he's spent the day at sea.

That hair in contrast with his black tailored trousers and starched white shirt give him a casual elegance, and it's easy to believe that this man is just as comfortable on a tennis court as he is in a boardroom.

His famous eyes capture my attention. They seem edgy and dangerous and full of dark promises. More important, they are watching me. Following me as I move toward him.

I feel an odd sense of déjà vu as I move steadily across the floor, hyperaware of my body, my posture, the placement of my feet. Foolishly, I feel as if I'm a contestant all over again.

I keep my eyes forward, not looking at his face. I don't like the nervousness that has crept into my manner. The sense that he can see beneath the armor I wear along with my little black dress.

One step, then another.

I can't help it; I look straight at him. Our eyes lock, and I swear all the air is sucked from the room. It is my old fantasy come to life, and I am completely lost. The sense of déjà vu vanishes and there's nothing but this moment, electric and powerful. *Sensual.*

For all I know, I've gone spinning off into space. But no, I'm right there, floor beneath me, walls around me, and Damien Stark's eyes on mine. I see heat and purpose. And then I see nothing but raw, primal desire so intense I fear that I'll shatter under the force of it.

Carl takes my elbow, steadying me, and only then do I realize I'd started to stumble. "Are you okay?"

"New shoes. Thanks." I glance back at Stark, but his eyes have gone flat. His mouth is a thin line. Whatever that was—and what the hell was it?—the moment has passed.

By the time we reach Stark, I've almost convinced myself it was my imagination.

I barely process the words as Evelyn introduces Carl. My turn is next, and Carl presses his hand to my shoulder, pushing me subtly forward. His palm is sweating, and it feels clammy against my bare skin. I force myself not to shrug it off.

"Nikki is Carl's new assistant," Evelyn says.

I extend my hand. "Nikki Fairchild. It's a pleasure." I don't mention that we've met before. Now hardly seems the time to remind him that I once paraded before him in a bathing suit.

"Ms. Fairchild," he says, ignoring my hand. My stomach twists, but I'm not sure if it's from nerves, disappointment, or anger. He looks from Carl to Evelyn, pointedly avoiding my eyes. "You'll have to excuse me. There's something I need to attend to right away." And then he's gone, swallowed up into the crowd as effectively as a magician disappearing in a puff of smoke.

"What the fuck?" Carl says, summing up my sentiments exactly.

Uncharacteristically quiet, Evelyn simply gapes at me, her expressive mouth turned down into a frown.

But I don't need words to know what she's

thinking. I can easily see that she's wondering the same thing I am: What just happened?

More important, what the hell did I do wrong?

3

My moment of mortification hangs over the three of us for what feels like an eternity. Then Carl takes my arm and begins to steer me away from Evelyn.

"Nikki?" Concern blooms in her eyes.

"I—it's okay," I say. I feel strangely numb and very confused. *This* is what I'd been looking forward to?

"I mean it, Nikki," Carl says, as soon as he's put some distance between us and our hostess. "What the fuck was that?"

"I don't know."

"Bullshit," he snaps. "Have you met before? Did you piss him off? Did you apply for a job with him before me? What the hell did you do, Nichole?"

I cringe against the use of my given name. "It's not me," I say, because I want that to be the truth. "He's famous. He's eccentric. He was rude, but it wasn't personal. How the hell could it have been?" I can hear my voice rising, and I force myself to tamp it down. To breathe.

I squeeze my left hand into a fist so tight my fingernails cut into my palm. I focus on the pain, on the simple process of breathing. I need to be cool. I need to be calm. I can't let the Social Nikki facade slip away.

Beside me, Carl runs his fingers through his hair and sucks in a noisy breath. "I need a drink. Come on."

"I'm fine, thanks." I am a long way from fine, but what I want right then is to be alone. Or as alone as I can be in a room full of people.

I can see that he wants to argue. I can also see that he hasn't yet decided what he's going to do. Approach Stark again? Leave the party and pretend it never happened? "Fine," he growls. He stalks off, and I can hear his muttered "Shit," as he disappears into the crowd.

I exhale, the tension in my shoulders slipping away. I head toward the balcony, but stop once I see that my private spot has been discovered. At least eight people mingle there, chatting and smiling. I am not in a chatty, smiley mood.

I veer toward one of the freestanding easels and stare blankly at the painting. It depicts a nude woman kneeling on a hard tile floor. Her arms are raised above her head, her wrists bound by a red ribbon.

The ribbon is attached to a chain that rises vertically out of the painting, and there is tension in her arms, as if she's tugging downward, trying to get free. Her stomach is smooth, her back arched so that the lines of her rib cage show. Her breasts are small, and the erect nipples and tight brown areolae glow under the artist's skill.

Her face is not so prominent. It's tilted away, shrouded in gray. I'm left with the impression that the model is ashamed of her arousal. That she would break free if she could. But she can't.

She's trapped there, her pleasure and her shame on display for all the world.

My own skin prickles and I realize that this girl and I have something in common. I'd felt a sensual power crash over me, and I'd reveled in it.

Then Stark had shut it off, as quickly as if he'd flipped a switch. And like that model I was left feeling awkward and ashamed.

Well, fuck him. That twit on the canvas might be embarrassed, but I wasn't going to be. I'd seen the heat in his eyes, and it had turned me on. Period. End of story. Time to move on.

I look hard at the woman on the canvas. She's weak. I don't like her, and I don't like the painting.

I start to move away, my own confidence restored—and I collide with none other than Damien Stark himself.

Well, shit.

His hand slides against my waist in an effort to steady me. I back away quickly, but not before my mind processes the feel of him. He's lean and hard, and I'm uncomfortably aware of the places where my body collided with his. My palm. My breasts.

The curve of my waist tingles from the lingering shock of his touch.

"Ms. Fairchild." He's looking straight at me, his eyes neither flat nor cold. I realize that I have stopped breathing.

I clear my throat and flash a polite smile. The kind that quietly says "Fuck off."

"I owe you an apology."

Oh.

"Yes," I say, surprised. "You do."

I wait, but he says nothing else. Instead, he turns his attention to the painting. "It's an interesting image. But you would have made a much better model."

What the ...?

"That's the worst apology I've ever heard."

He indicates the model's face. "She's weak," he says, and I forget all about the apology. I'm too intrigued by the way his words echo my earlier thoughts. "I suppose some people might be drawn to the contrast. Desire and shame. But I prefer something bolder. A more confident sensuality."

He looks at me as he says this last, and I'm not sure if he's finally apologizing for snubbing me, complimenting my composure, or being completely inappropriate. I decide to consider his words a compliment and go from there. It may not be the safest approach, but it's the most flattering.

"I'm delighted you think so," I say. "But I'm not the model type."

He takes a step back and with slow deliberation looks me up and down. His inspection seems to last for hours, though it must take only seconds. The air between us crackles, and I want to move toward him, to close the gap between us again. But I stay rooted to the spot.

He lingers for a moment on my lips before finally lifting his head to meet my eyes, and that is when I move. I can't help it. I'm drawn in by the force and pressure of the tempest building in those damnable eyes.

"No," he says simply.

At first I'm confused, thinking that he's protesting my proximity. Then I realize he's responding to my comment about not being the model type.

"You are," he continues. "But not like this—splashed across a canvas for all the world to see, belonging to no one and everyone." His head tilts slightly to the left, as if he's trying out a new perspective on me. "No," he murmurs again, but this time he doesn't elaborate.

I am not prone to blushing, and I'm mortified to realize that my cheeks are burning. For someone who just a few moments ago mentally told this man to fuck off, I am doing a piss-poor job of keeping the upper hand. "I was hoping to have the chance to talk to you this evening," I say.

His brow lifts ever so slightly, giving him an expression of polite amusement. "Oh?"

"I'm one of your fellowship recipients. I wanted to say thank you."

He doesn't say a word.

I soldier on. "I worked my way through college, so the fellowship helped tremendously. I don't think I could have graduated with two degrees if it hadn't been for the financial help. So thank you." I still don't mention the pageant. As far as I'm concerned, Damien Stark and I are deep in the land of the do-over.

"And what are you doing now that you've left the hallowed halls of academia?"

He speaks so formally that I know he's teasing me. I ignore it and answer the question seriously. "I joined the team at C-Squared," I say. "I'm Carl Rosenfeld's new assistant." Evelyn already told him this, but I assume he hadn't been paying attention.

"I see."

The way he says it suggests he doesn't see at all. "Is that a problem?"

"Two degrees. A straight-A average. Glowing recommendations from all your professors. Acceptance to Ph.D. programs at both MIT and Cal Tech."

I stare at him, baffled. The Stark International Fellowship Committee awards thirty fellowships each year. How the hell can he possibly know so much about my academic career?

"I merely find it interesting that you ended up

not leading a product development team but doing gruntwork as the owner's assistant."

"I—" I don't know what to say. I'm still spinning from the surreal nature of this inquisition.

"Are you sleeping with your boss, Ms. Fairchild?"

"*What?*"

"I'm sorry. Was the question unclear? I asked if you were fucking Carl Rosenfeld."

"I—*no.*" I blurt the answer out, because I can't let that image linger for longer than a second. Immediately, though, I regret speaking. What I should have done was slap his face. What the *hell* kind of question is that?

"Good," he says, so crisply and firmly and with such intensity that any thought I have of verbally bitch-slapping him vanishes completely. My thoughts, in fact, have taken a sharp left turn and I am undeniably, unwelcomely turned on. I glare at the woman in the portrait, hating her even more, and not particularly pleased with Damien Stark or myself. I suppose we have something in common, though. At the moment, we're both picturing me out of my little black dress.

Shit.

He doesn't even try to hide his amusement. "I believe I've shocked you, Ms. Fairchild."

"Hell yes, you've shocked me. What did you expect?"

He doesn't answer, just tilts his head back and

laughs. It's as if a mask has slipped away, allowing me a glimpse of the real man hidden beneath. I smile, liking that we have this one small thing in common.

"Can anyone join this party?" It's Carl, and I want desperately to say no.

"How nice to see you again, Mr. Rosenfeld," Stark says. The mask is firmly back in place.

Carl glances at me, and I can see the question in his eyes. "Excuse me," I say. "I need to run to the ladies' room."

I escape to the cool elegance of Evelyn's powder room. She's thoughtfully provided mouthwash and hairspray and even disposable mascara wands. There is a lavender-scented salt scrub on the stone vanity, and I put a spoonful in my hands, then close my eyes and rub, imagining that I'm sloughing off the shell of myself to reveal something bright and shiny and new.

I rinse my hands in warm water, then caress my skin with my fingertips. My hands are soft now. Slick and sensual.

I meet my eyes in the mirror. "No," I whisper, but my hand slides down to brush the hem of my dress just below my knee. It's fitted at the bodice and waist, but the skirt is flared, designed to present an enticing little swish when you move.

My fingers dance across my knee, then trail lazily up my inner thigh. I meet my gaze in the mirror, then close my eyes. It's Stark's face I want to see. His eyes I imagine watching me from that mirror.

There's a sensuality in the way my fingers slowly graze my own skin. A lazy eroticism that some other time could build to something hot and explosive. But that's not where I'm going—that's what I'm destroying.

I stop when I feel it—the jagged, raised tissue of the five-year-old scar that mars the once-perfect flesh of my inner thigh. I press my fingertips to it, remembering the pain that punctuated that particular wound. That had been the weekend that my sister, Ashley, had died, and I'd just about crumbled under the weight of my grief.

But that's the past, and I close my eyes tight, my body hot, the scar throbbing beneath my hand.

This time when I open my eyes, all I see is myself. Nikki Fairchild, back in control.

I wrap my restored confidence around me like a blanket and return to the party. Both men look at me as I approach. Stark's face is unreadable, but Carl isn't even trying to hide his joy. He looks like a six-year-old on Christmas morning. "Say your goodbyes, Nikki. We're heading out. Lots to do. *Lots* to do."

"What? Now?" I don't bother to hide my confusion.

"Turns out Mr. Stark's going to be out of town on Tuesday, so we're pushing the meeting to tomorrow."

"Saturday?"

"Is that a problem?" Stark asks me.

"No, of course not, but—"

"He's attending personally," Carl says. "Personally," he repeats, as if I could have missed it the first time.

"Right. I'll just find Evelyn and say goodnight." I start to move away, but Stark's voice draws me back.

"I'd like Ms. Fairchild to stay."

"What?" Carl speaks, expressing my thought.

"The house I'm building is almost complete. I came here to find a painting for a particular room. I'd like a feminine perspective. I'll see her home safely, of course."

"Oh." Carl looks like he's going to protest, then thinks better of it. "She'll be happy to help."

The hell she will. It's one thing to wear the dress. It's another to completely skip the presentation rehearsal because a self-absorbed bazillionaire snaps his fingers and says jump. No matter how hot said bazillionaire might be.

But Carl cuts me off before I can form a coherent reply. "We'll speak tomorrow morning," he tells me. "The meeting's at two."

And then he's gone and I'm left seething beside a very smug Damien Stark.

"Who the hell do you think you are?"

"I know exactly who I am, Ms. Fairchild. Do you?"

"Maybe the better question is, who the hell do you think *I* am?"

"Are you attracted to me?"

"I—what?" I say, verbally stumbling. His words have knocked me off center, and I struggle to regain my balance. "That is so not the issue."

The corner of his mouth twitches, and I realize I've revealed too much.

"I'm Carl's assistant," I say firmly and slowly. "Not yours. And my job description does not include decorating your goddamn house." I'm not shouting, but my voice is as taut as a wire and my body even more so.

Stark, damn him, appears not only perfectly at ease, but also completely amused. "If your job duties include helping your boss find capital, then you may want to reconsider how you play the game. Insulting potential investors is probably not the best approach."

A cold stab of fear that I've screwed this up cuts through me. "Maybe not," I say. "But if you're going to withhold your money because I didn't roll over and flounce my skirts for you, then you're not the man the press makes you out to be. The Damien Stark I've read about invests in quality. Not in friendships or relationships or because he thinks some poor little inventor needs the deal. The Damien Stark I admire focuses on talent and talent alone. Or is that just public relations?"

I stand straight, ready to endure whatever

verbal lashes he'll whip back at me. I'm not prepared for the response I get.

Stark laughs.

"You're right," he says. "I'm not going to invest in C-Squared because I met Carl at a party any more than I'd invest in it because you're in my bed."

"Oh." Once again, my cheeks heat. Once again, he's knocked me off balance.

"I do, however, want you."

My mouth is dry. I have to swallow before I can speak. "To help you pick a painting?"

"Yes," he confirms. "For now."

I force myself not to wonder about later. "Why?"

"Because I need an honest opinion. Most women on my arm say what they think will make me happy, not what they actually mean."

"But I'm not on your arm, Mr. Stark." I let the words hang for a moment. Then I deliberately turn my back and walk away. I can feel him watching me, but I neither stop nor turn around. Slowly, I smile. I even add a little swing to my step. This is my moment of triumph and I intend to savor it.

Except victory isn't as delicious as I expected. In fact, it's a little bitter. Because secretly—oh, so secretly—I can't help but wonder what it would be like to be the girl on Damien Stark's arm.

ABOUT THE AUTHOR

J. Kenner (aka Julie Kenner) is the *New York Times*, *USA Today*, *Publishers Weekly*, *Wall Street Journal* and #1 International bestselling author of over one hundred novels, novellas and short stories in a variety of genres.

JK has been praised by *Publishers Weekly* as an author with a "flair for dialogue and eccentric characterizations" and by *RT Bookclub* for having "cornered the market on sinfully attractive, dominant antiheroes and the women who swoon for them." A five-time finalist for Romance Writers of America's prestigious RITA award, JK took home the first RITA trophy awarded in the category of erotic romance in 2014 for her novel, *Claim Me* (book 2 of her Stark Trilogy) and the RITA trophy for *Wicked Dirty* in the same category in 2017.

In her previous career as an attorney, JK worked as a lawyer in Southern California and Texas. She currently lives in Central Texas, with her husband, two daughters, and two rather spastic cats.

Visit her website at www.juliekenner.com to learn more and to connect with JK through social media!

Made in the USA
Monee, IL
27 April 2022